Part I

I. Genesis

Laying on a patterned antique rug positioned in the centre of an ordinary, rectangular-shaped room was a girl. The girl had golden blond hair and pretty, delicate features such as a small and rounded nose and lightly-coloured eyebrows. In spite of her somewhat youthful characteristics, the girl was unmistakably a woman, likely in her mid to late twenties. She had dull pink lips that were faintly creased, matching her dull pink cheeks and very lightly wrinkled forehead. The girl was undoubtedly attractive, roughly average height and build, and was dressed rather unassumingly, with an aura of innocence and unknowing about her.

Her eyes opened sharply to reveal deep blue irises and intensely black pupils that after a momentary pause quickly darted from left to right, scanning the ceiling of the room. After noticing nothing of interest, the girl abruptly shot upright into a sitting position, with her legs still outstretched and her arms supporting her weight from behind. Abruptly she was startled by an inconspicuous looking cat, sitting directly opposite her on the floor, with its back to the wall. For a few seconds the girl engaged in a staring contest with the innocent-looking black and white creature, holding her gaze directly into its sharp green eyes. It appeared as though they were both attempting to suss each other out. Eventually the cat casually sauntered over to the girl, and affectionately brushed its body up against the girl's denim-covered left thigh. The cat's fur was soft, even more so than the woollen rug her palms were pressing down on. The cat's benevolent nature put the girl's anxiety to ease at once, allowing her to analyse the room in more detail.

She scoured the scantly decorated room with a mildly puzzled look on her face, yet did not seem too intimidated or shocked by the situation she found herself in. To the right of her she noticed a large wooden door, well-polished from hinge to handle, with one small central crown glass window allowing a surprising and pleasant amount of daylight into the room. The girl began scanning the room from right to left, noticing that in the adjacent wall, the wall that the girl was directly facing, was a tall, narrow archway that seemed to lead to a corridor of sorts. Continuing her hastily inquisitive scan of the room, she noticed another wooden door to her left, similar to the first door, but smaller. The door was invitingly ajar. With little else to remark about the room the girl climbed to her feet. As soon as she put her bodyweight onto her legs she wobbled, almost collapsing back to the floor. Her legs felt weak and felt jelly-like, and in that moment she felt an unsettling unfamiliarity within her body. Her hands were imprinted with a satisfying pattern created from resting her bodyweight on them while perched up on the rug on the floor. A few seconds after her minor stumble she was able to compose herself, and with full feeling re-entering her legs she was able to turn to look at the wall behind her – the only wall she was yet to inspect. While trying to ignore the on-rushing paraesthesia of her lower legs and feet, she observed a third doorway, this time more rustic and antique, with a mediaeval-looking stone door frame. Immediately this doorway intrigued her the most out of everything she had seen so far, and she felt herself being physically drawn to it with an inner sense of virtuous curiosity. But before she could even begin to fulfil this feeling, a mild ringing in her ears grabbed her focus instead. The ringing sensation, of which she now realised had been there the whole time, quickly faded and left behind a gentle noise of sporadic tip-tapping of what the girl thought to be pots and pans.

The sound was coming from behind the door that had been left ajar. Almost subconsciously the girl's curiosity brought her closer to the door. As if to seal the fate of the girl's next move, she spotted the cat that had been sitting by her feet since she stood up, canter towards the doorway, before sharply turning left, squeezing through the gap in the door. There was now little stopping the girl from approaching the suggestively ajar door. As she got within a meter or so of the door she recognised the additional sound of movement, presumably human movement, also coming from beyond the door. Her awareness of this made her infinitely more hesitant than she previously was, however she continued to creep towards the door. Once the door was within reach, she gently grabbed the open side of the door with both hands and attempted to peer around the door as covertly as possible. It took a short while for her eyes to adjust to the bright rays of sunlight beaming across the room, before her vision focused on an average height, slightly plump man, dressed mostly in white and wearing what appeared to be a chef's hat. Half of the girl's mind prompted her to immediately recoil out of view of the man, but this was seemingly overridden by the other half of her mind, which had noted his inherently disarming nature. With a perhaps surprising lack of hesitation, the girl stepped out from behind the door while opening it fully, and uttered, "Hello?" in an unsure tone. Her voice was hoarse and she subsequently cleared her throat.

"Good morning," the man quickly responded, without looking up from the wooden counter-top in front of him, upon which he was currently preparing vegetables in a leisurely manner. He seemed rather content with what he was doing, while simultaneously providing a feeling of friendliness, equal to the warming ambiance of the room. He had medium-length curly brown hair poking out from the sides of the chef's hat, and soft, indistinct features to his face.

"Who are you?" the girl inquired, tentatively awaiting a response for what felt like an eternity, to no avail. The man continued to wash and slice vegetables without any sign of acknowledgement of the question.

"Hello?" the girl said again, this time slightly more assertively.

"Good morning, how are you this morning?" the man calmly and sincerely responded.

"Who are you and where am I?" the girl, ignoring his question, hurriedly but politely questioned. Again the man did not respond, and there was not so much as a slight change of expression on his face, which remained calm and friendly-looking. The girl waited briefly, before appearing to attempt to calculate the situation, and change approach.

"What are you doing?" she asked.

"I'm just preparing some vegetables for dinner this evening," the man replied, again with a sincere and friendly confidence.

"Dinner for who?" she speedily questioned in response.

"For everyone," he equivocated.

The girl examined the room around with an intrigued expression, taking a couple of timid steps through the doorway into the room, while partially expecting to see other people in the room that she had not yet noticed. The room was a large, open-plan kitchen-diner, resembling that of a 90's-style cottage kitchen-diner, but much more spacious. Most of the surfaces were made of wood, including a long floating island at which the man was preparing the vegetables, and a charming wooden dining table, positioned under an expansive set of bay windows that covered almost the entirety of the left wall of the room. Through the windows was a small, inviting Eden-esque garden consisting of luscious green plants and fruit-bearing trees and bushes. Caught almost spellbound by the scene, the girl remembered what the man had said, about making dinner for 'everyone'. She re-engaged with her scan of the room, but there was certainly no one else there with them, nor was there even an indication that someone else had been there recently.

"Where am I?" the girl probed again, trying her luck for the second time. Her question was met with a similar lack of acknowledgement and subsequent silence as before. "Why won't you answer my questions?" she queried the man again, with a growing hint of frustration about her.

"Sorry, I am just preparing dinner for everyone," the man replied. Despite the girl's growing frustration the man's calmness did not deteriorate in the slightest.

"Who is 'everyone'?" the girl questioned.

"Everyone else in the house," the man responded. There was a nervous silence while the girl attempted to make sense of what was going on, but before she could interrogate the man further, he, for the first time yet, looked up from his chopping board and relaxed the grip on his knife slightly.

"They will likely be in their rooms, if you want to go and see them," he urged, now looking directly at the girl standing opposite him. He let out an affectionate smile towards the girl. As creepy and confusing as the situation may have seemed, the girl did not feel as nearly on-edge as she could have. Although she was moderately scared, and understandably so, she had not yet encountered the urge to run or scream for help, not in the slightest. Instead, partly through frustration with the lack of response she was getting from the man, she decided to fulfil his suggestion, and turned around one hundred and eighty degrees, striding back into the room she had come from previously. After turning around, the big wooden door with the small circular window instantaneously grabbed her attention. She had immediately, at least for the time being, forgotten about going to find these other people that the chef had promised existed elsewhere in the house. She strode towards the door, now at the centre of her attention, and grasped the handle with intent. In one clean motion she opened the door, the metal handle turning smoothly without a shred of resistance, as if it were brand new.

As the girl stepped outside into the lukewarm Goldilock-temperature air, she recognised the true abnormality of her surroundings. In front of her was no more than a few meters of ground, consisting primarily of enticing deep green grass, a couple of inches in length, and a crudely quaint gravel path that came right up to the front door of the house. Beyond the ground in front of her was, well… nothing? She immediately tread towards the edge of the grounded area she could see in front of her to inspect what was beyond it. With each step she detected the thousands of mildly jagged pieces of grey gravel making up the path beneath her bare feet, but this did not seem to cause her much discomfort. The closer she got to the edge, the more disappointed she became with the realisation that her initial assumption about the edge of the land was correct – there was nothing beyond it. Somewhat bewildered, she peered over the edge, seeing only sky and clouds beneath. They were the sort of perfectly formed, white fluffy clouds that you would imagine to see in only the most idyllic of places, such as at the gates to heaven, and were approximately one hundred foot beneath the girl, she estimated. She traced the edge of the land round with her eyes, first to her right, where she noticed a significant yet compact crop farm, enclosed by a pristine-looking wooden fence that stood at about waist-height. Behind some of the shorter crops that were not blocking her field of vision, she was able to observe a tiny farmer's hut, with a corrugated tin roof and vertical overlapping strips of wood making up its walls. She then turned to face to her left, again tracing the edge of the land along, slowly. On this side there was not much to be seen, merely a few pleasant looking hedges and bushes either side of the gravel path that continued on around the back of the house. The girl concluded from what she had so far observed that she must be on some sort of floating island. The speed at which she came to accept this hypothesis made her second-guess her own sanity for a brief period of time. At this moment she forced herself to stop and question what on earth was going on and where on earth she was. It was in this instant that she also came to the humbling and daunting realisation that she did not even know *who* she was.

The girl's stomach sank – like she had swallowed an anvil. She was now undoubtedly scared. Quickly, however, she was able to compose herself for a second time. Seemingly as though she had acquired experience via similar ordeals previously (although she had surely never experienced anything conceivably close to this), she was able to relax enough to turn herself around, and with a half determined and half petrified look about her face, she began purposefully walking back toward the house. Although she was walking with enthusiastic strides, she did not yet have an understanding, or even an idea, of where she was going next. She lunged through the door, which was still wide open, and stepped onto the tightly bristled welcome mat that provided a slight tickling sensation on the soles of her feet. She froze once again, appearing understandably perplexed and indecisive, when, as if by magic, the black and white cat scampered out from the kitchen towards the girl and through the archway in the wall to the girl's right. As the cat darted through the archway its tail made a singular muted knocking noise as it collided with the plain white wall of the archway. Completing its U-shaped path, the cat nimbly turned back on itself and shot off down the comparatively dimly-lit corridor. Once again the girl saw no reason not to follow the cat. By the time she had stepped foot into the corridor however, the cat was out of sight, presumably having entered one of the two more archways that the corridor presented. The corridor was just as plain as the front room, having only bare mahogany walls, and two protruding oval-shaped lights positioned in even increments along the ceiling. In fact, the only other aesthetic detail the girl could discern was the immaculately painted bright white skirting boards that had a yellowish tinge and glow emanating from them under the artificial light. The floor in the corridor was carpeted, which was a welcomed change to the soles of the girl's feet. While still being uninspiring in appearance, the light blue carpet was velvety smooth, and it only further encouraged the girl's subconscious into exploring the corridor. Roughly half way down the hallway, on the right-hand side was the first of the two other archways. It was very similar to, if not exactly the same as the one she had just entered the corridor from. From it, a radiant glow of sunlight was attempting to spill out into the corridor. It was inviting, but in the given context of the situation it was also quite unnerving. It was however not as unnerving as the archway at the very end of the corridor, directly in front of the girl at around fifteen paces or so in distance. Through the archway, simply darkness. It appeared to lead to a completely dark room, of which the girl could not pick out a single feature from the other end of the corridor at which she was standing. It made sense then, not only logistically, but also for the sake of the girl's nervousness, to focus for the time being on the first archway, roughly seven to eight paces away, in the wall on the girl's right. She tentatively stepped towards the sunlight creeping out of the archway, while trying to convince herself mentally of the positive outcomes she hoped would come about from her decision to explore. She also acknowledged within herself that there was a certain inevitability about her bravery – 'What else is there that I can do?' she thought to herself, reassuringly. Although her approach to the archway was timid, there was a simultaneous air of rectitude in her bravery, almost as though she had an inner voice reinforcing to her the idea that it was the right thing to do. Before she had travelled far enough to see clearly into the room beyond the archway, the sunlight that was reflecting off of the similarly plain white walls of the room to her right hit the top of her bare feet, providing an almost euphoric warming feeling that seemed to swallow her feet whole, almost making her feel at home, at least for a brief moment. As she got closer to the archway the gratifying warmth of the reflected sunlight gradually rose up her legs. She could now see that on the left-hand wall of the room was a set of shelves. Three shelves positioned one above the other, with the lowest one hanging at roughly chest-height to the girl. Similar to the gleaming skirting boards of the corridor, they were immaculately painted white, and were bearing the weight of not so much as a speck of dust. 'Why is this place so bare?' she thought to herself while stepping onto the glossy dark wooden panel on the floor that divided the carpet of the corridor and the floorboards of the room, which had also been kept warm by the sunlight. Having repeated this step with her trailing right foot, the souls of her feet were now experiencing three different textures. Her heels were still seemingly floating on the pillow-like carpet of the corridor, while the bulk of the soles of her feet were being gently warmed by the well-polished dark wood partition, that was almost but not quite flush with the carpet, and the very tips of her toes could just about feel the slightly less glossy and cooler nature of the floorboards of the room. Her mind however was swiftly snapped out of its focus on these sensations when she noticed another man, laying out flat on his back on an antique sofa that matched the style of the large rugs in both the front room and this room, positioned under more large bay windows on the right-hand side wall of the room, the wall running parallel to the wall supporting the empty shelves. With a pillow marginally propping up his bearded and long-haired head, the man peacefully laid on the sofa with his eyes closed, with a complete lack of acknowledgement of the girl's presence. Although his appearance was most certainly unkempt, the man, dressed in an old white shirt and dark grey blazer upon his torso and grey baggy tracksuit bottoms upon his legs, did not seem to be dirty or to be significantly lacking personal hygiene, beyond his vaguely straggly and greasy black hair. His assuredly worn-in but still fairly well polished black leather shoes completed his amusingly literal smart-casual outfit. If it weren't for the opened long draping opal-blue patterned curtains letting in the radiant sunlight, and the smooth stone fireplace with a rustic brick border that followed on to form the chimney breast above it in the wall opposite the archway in which the girl was still standing, this could have been quite a dingy and depressing scene. As the man, who she assumed to be deep in sleep, appeared to be of no threat to the girl whatsoever, she allowed herself a short visual inspection of the room. Without even a slight hint of movement, so as to not disturb the unknown man, the girl observed that around the fireplace were six comfortable looking seats, varying in colours and style. Some were small armchairs, matching the style of the sofa and rug, while others were more stool-like, some three-legged and some with four wooden legs. They were positioned around the fireplace, each with an equal view of it, rather perfectly, presumably intentionally so. This was in keeping with the rest of the house that she had seen so far, in which everything appeared meticulously clean and approaching ritualistic in its positioning. The girl's gaze floated up towards the clock above the fireplace. The clock was simple in design; circular with a grey metal border and opaquely printed, or perhaps painted, black roman numerals behind its thin transparent shallow dome-shaped glass. Both hands of the clock were pointing precisely to 'XII', and did not appear to be moving. The girl held her gaze for a few seconds, expecting the hands to move, but they did not. Suddenly, she was made to jump, nearly off her feet, in shock.

"The clocks don't work," mumbled the man lying on the sofa, begrudgingly.

The girl was shaken by this unexpected, although very muffled, comment from the man. She had to take a moment to get her breath back, which had been stolen from her by her inescapable momentary panic. With a slight tremble in her voice still, she gave the man a response.

"What do you mean the clocks don't work?" she queried.

"They don't work, none of them do, never have," he replied, lazily, ending with a short sigh demonstrating his lack of enthusiasm for the conversation.

"Why don't they work?" the girl swiftly quizzed back.

"Mmm... you'll find out... probably," he responded, finishing by letting out a slothful yawn, still with his eyes casually and unpretentiously closed. Of course, the girl was very confused by this. Having had enough of the man's idleness and disinterest in the conversation, compounded with the apparent distress that the conversation, the man, and this room were causing her, the girl decided to turn around and head back out into the corridor to explore a different part of the house. She knew wholeheartedly that there was a good chance she would be forced to return to question the man later on, as he seemed to have some knowledge that could potentially offer some answers to the plentiful questions that were reverberating around inside her head, the most pressing of which being '*where* the fuck am I?' and '*who* the fuck am I?'. She consolidated her decision to leave the room by reasoning with herself that the man may be in a more willingly cooperative state when, or if, she returned.

Her erratic footsteps on the soft blue carpet of the corridor produced miniature echoes, the sound of which the girl pondered about how far it could travel in this eerily quiet house. As she steadily approached the second archway, the one leading to the ominous darkness, she began to consider the possibility that her approaching presence could be audible to whoever, or whatever, awaited her. This feeling of walking into the unknown, completely exposed to the ghastly possibilities of the portal-like black archway made her feel particularly vulnerable. She stood still, almost frozen, close to the archway, outwardly attempting to hype herself up into action, when she heard a gentle 'Meow' come from the darkness, cutting through the trepidatious silence like a tiny beacon of light into a pitch-black sky, as if the cat were somehow consciously attempting to help calm the girl's nerves and encourage her to enter the room. It was followed by delicate licking noises, the sound of the cat licking the fur on its legs. Clear as crystal, the sound reached the girl in her otherwise silent surroundings, and made her feel infinitely more relaxed. Attempting to use this more relaxed state to her benefit, and without much more thought, she thrust her left arm around the right side of the archway in one sweeping motion, in the hope of finding a light switch. Surprisingly, the girl managed to land her index finger immediately on a light switch on the inside of the right-hand side of the wall that the archway was cut out of, and in the same one motion she flicked it on. The girl was too caught up in her situation, understandably, to consider what had just happened. Was it just pure luck that the light switch had been exactly where she flung her left hand in hope? Or was her subconscious somehow aware of the location of the light switch in the room? And if so, how?

Bam! The inverted dish-shaped light hanging from the ceiling of the room turned on, exploding bright incandescent light throughout the room in an eye-watering fashion. Once the girl's eyes had sufficiently adjusted to the overbearing light reflecting off of the again completely uninspiring plain mahogany walls, a mild disappointment fell upon her. Another empty room. This time, a near-perfect square in shape, and with its only notable feature being yet more doors and archways. 'Great,' she thought, sarcastically, to herself, 'more terrifying doors to go through'. Although she was partially relieved that nothing sinister was waiting for her in the room, she couldn't help being a little frustrated with the lack of, well... anything. The cat, sitting on the blue carpet that continued into the room from the corridor, stared at her again, as if to be mocking her, affectionately. She could already see from where she was standing that the archway in the wall to the right of her just led to another corridor.

"What is this, some kind of maze?" she whispered quietly to herself, potentially not even aware that she had said the words out loud. Her puzzlement and frustration was clearly growing in equal measures. Then, to the girl's startlement, the rustic spherical black metal doorknob of the door in the middle of the wall on her left turned, and with it the painted white door opened, revealing a glimpse of a deep red wall on the inside of another room. 'Finally, some colour,' the girl thought to herself. Unsure if due to simply the enticing nature of the deep red colour, or if it was something more, the girl felt a certain giddiness in her stomach, a miniature kaleidoscope of butterflies. This, of course, could be simply a feeling of pure dread and anxiety, infiltrating her body and mind like a Trojan horse. Nevertheless the girl did not have time to contemplate this, as from the room confidently stepped another girl. The girl had shoulder-length straight black hair with a neat full fringe and full pink lips, dressed in a V-neck buttoned black top and a slightly above knee-length loose-fitting ruffled red skirt, echoing the colour of the wall behind her, and being held up by a stylish thin black belt around her waist. The girls appeared to admire one-another's beauty for a split second, perhaps more in acknowledgement than awe.

"Hi," the dark-haired girl announced, in a voice that was evidently constituted of both excitement and mild embarrassment. She leaned her left shoulder against the inside of the door frame, while crossing her left leg back behind her right, resting only the toes of her left foot on the floor.

"Um... Hi?" the blonde-haired girl replied, apprehensively.

"Would you like me to show you around?" the girl asked. Her lips burst into a friendly smile.

"Where am I?" the blonde-haired girl probed, once again, hoping that the third time was indeed a charm. She reciprocated the girl's friendliness, allowing for her now moderately chapped lips to form into a stifled smile.

"That's not really for me to tell you, I'm sorry," the girl responded. Her warm complexion in parallel with her friendly mannerisms created an almost tangible physical heat, radiating from her like a fluorescent glow under UV light. The blonde-haired girl frowned slightly, but she was becoming accustomed to this sort of disappointing reluctance to divulge meaningful answers to her questions that the people of this house seemed to collectively possess. "So, how about that tour?" the dark-haired girl followed up with, swiftly, not leaving much time for the blonde-haired girl to dwell on the matter.

"Sure," she said back, "So far I've only had this little fellow showing me around," she sniggered shyly, pointing to the floor to her right where the cat had earlier been sitting. However, when she turned her head the cat was gone, without even one visible piece of fur left to be seen. The girl experienced slight embarrassment that the cat was no longer there and the fact that she was in fact now merely pointing at a vacant patch of blue carpet. She hoped, *at least,* that the cat had actually been real, and that she hadn't just imagined it. Although that currently wouldn't surprise her, taking into consideration how her day had gone up to this point.

"It's okay, you didn't imagine him," the dark-haired girl interjected. "He doesn't often stay in one room for a long amount of time, itchy feet," she added, with a giggle. She looked at the blonde-haired girl in the eyes, meaningfully. 'How did she know I was thinking that?' the blonde-haired girl remarked to herself internally. 'It must have been obvious, I suppose,' she reasoned with her own inner dialogue. 'I need to try and relax or else this is going to be a really long fucking day,' she rallied to herself, again internally. It was at this moment that she also noticed just how wonderfully the dark-haired girl smelt. Her delightfully fragrant and floral perfume emanated from every part of her, from head to toe to slender olive-tinted fingertip. The blonde-haired girl looked back toward the dark-haired girl and smiled, politely, patiently awaiting the inception of the tour she had been promised.

"Okay, so obviously this is my room," said the girl, pointing back at the room behind her with outstretched arms. "As you can tell, I like to paint," the girl asserted. The blonde-haired girl peered around the doorway into the girl's room. Numerous beautifully painted pieces of art were hung, glued and stapled across her walls, arranged in a delightfully flowing scene. Varying in content from generic landscape scene to tantalisingly provocative moderate erotica, the girl found these paintings captivating, especially in contrast with the depressingly minimal amount of expressionism she had seen throughout the rest of the house so far. Two of the walls of the room were painted in the aforementioned deep red colour, glossy and mildly seductive. The other two were, unfortunately yet predictably, white. The room had a large double bed, made with a pretty deep black silken duvet and pillow set. The bed was positioned in the far left corner of the room, with the silken red curtains that matched the glossy walls hanging either side of the window on the back wall above the pillow end of the bed. It was a small, comforting room, the bed taking up approximately half of the floor space on its own. Through the double windows above the bed the view was limited. Only the right-hand side of a generously fruit-bearing apple tree and what was presumably the edge of this unfathomable floating island could be discerned from the doorway to the room in which the girl was standing. The girl's gaze was lost for a moment on the tempting snake-skinned barked tree, before a bubble of thought simultaneously appeared and popped inside her head, 'I haven't even asked her name, how rude of me'. At once she snapped out of her trance.

"Sorry to interrupt," she spurted. "What's your name?" she asked, optimistically. The inherent connection between the two of them seemed to be growing with every word shared and every piece of body language, although the blond-haired girl's understandable apprehension managed to significantly limit its flourish.

"Libidine," the dark-haired girl turned and affirmed. "But you can call me Libi", she stated, again offering a reassuring smile.

"And, urr… What's my name?" the blonde-haired girl queried back, hesitantly.

"Again this is not for me to tell you, and in fact I may not even know your name, and why should it matter if I do?" Libi responded, jovially. The riddle-like response left the blonde-haired girl with a rather riddle-induced expression on her face, yet she remained calm. As she had internally agreed with herself earlier, she was committed to maintain her superiority over her emotions for as long as she could, in aid of finding out objectively what was going on here. Besides, she was happy enough that the girl had at least offered her something, a name, by which she felt encouraged.

"Anyway," Libi interrupted the girl's train of thought, ushering the girl back through the doorway to the room. "And then this here is your room," she announced, pointing, again with outstretched arms, towards the closed door in the wall to the left of the room they had just exited. The door was identical to the one to Libi's room – plain, white, spherical black metal doorknob.

"My room?" the girl immediately blurted back.

"Yes, your room," Libi reiterated, calmly. With a few reassuringly confident strides, she led the girl to the door, the footsteps of her (also bare) feet reverberating around the room in an identical fashion to the girl's. 'How can I have a room here?' she thought to herself, 'I've never seen this place before, it doesn't make any sense'. With their strides and footsteps twinned in uncanny synchronisation, the girl followed, a cacophony of questions ricocheting about inside her head like oppositely-charged atoms. In a rapid fashion her anxiety grew, with her narrowing proximity to the door acting as a strong catalyst. 'Is this a trap?' she questioned to herself, 'This could easily be a trap,' her panic continued to intensify, exponentially. Upon the penultimate stride toward the doorway the floorboards beneath the carpet uttered a sinister creak, making the hairs on the girls arms, legs and neck stand on end, the rest of the house still unnervingly silent. Even Libi now appeared devoid of noise, and the girl's all-encompassing fear almost entirely drowned out Libi's previously unignorably wonderful perfumed scent. The girl did not know why, not at all, but she had a bad feeling about this room. She watched on, a couple of paces behind Libi, frozen in trepidation, as Libi clasped the doorknob, her supple palm and fingers surrounding the cold metal without hesitation. She turned the knob promptly, yet it seemed to the girl to take a short eternity, her mind and eyes now completely focused on the unisonous clockwise rotation of the doorknob and Libi's hand and wrist.

Libi opened the door steadily, revealing a relatively large but not in any way menacing bedroom. Directly in front of the door in the middle of the room was a comfortable looking bed made with a pretty blue patterned duvet and pillow set. The wall directly behind the bed was decorated with a welcoming gold, blue, black and white wallpaper depicting a flowing array of trees, mushrooms and birds. Golden accents dotted throughout the depictions twinkled in the girl's eyes. A little less frightened and intrigued by the room, the girl stepped forward into the doorway. The room had a neutral smell, or at least it was neutral to the girl, as, perhaps, it smelt like her. It was quite dark, only the pleasant glow of a small lamp on a dainty raw-wood bedside stand. This was because the window, to her left, was currently covered by large blackout curtains, prohibiting even the slightest bit of sunlight from entering the room. The girl stood and watched, trying to analyse the little detail she could discern about the room, as Libi walked over to the bedside stand, her strides still consistently fearless. She switched off the light, leaving them both in near complete darkness, but for the mere meters-worth of light that eked itself into the room from the hallway. The girl's heart rate began to rise again, she could no longer see or hear Libi at all, what was she doing? Was this the trap? She clung to the doorframe, even scratching some of the paint off of it with her nails, in the hope of ensuring the door could not close behind her. Two to three seconds passed without a single peep of sound or sign of movement from Libi at the back of the dark room.

Schwing! Daylight burst into the room from the girl's left like water from an enormous bursting dam.

"That's better," Libi emphasised. She had enthusiastically flung the heavy curtains apart, with left and right side parting emphatically, in near-perfect symmetry. The open curtains revealed a charming view of the garden and section of the farm area. The apple tree partly visible from Libi's window was in full view at the foreground of the picturesque scene, framed in situ by the ornate blue window frame. On the opposite wall to the girl's right, the sunlight had illuminated a narrow tall bookcase, empty, and a similarly ornate raw-wood desk, in keeping with the style of the rest of the room. The girl noted a sense of familiarity about the room. She appreciated the decoration, all to her taste. She took one brave apprehensive step onto the cream-coloured carpet, which felt *even* softer to her bare soles than the delightfully fleecy carpet of the hallway and corridor. No sooner had she made a singular timid step into the room than her surprising familiarity and comfort within it quickly began to fade in prominence. Anxiety and fear, which had by no means disappeared, began an overwhelming resurgence over her body. The room made her feel something, with a strong force. She felt in some way connected to the room.

She considered that she may be mistaking an overpoweringly strong feeling as a negative one, and that in fact it may be more neutral in nature, or that it was even possible that what she was experiencing could even potentially be some twisted manifestation of euphoria? Nevertheless, the feeling was undeniable, and it was resulting in wave after wave of intensifying paranoia, anxiety and fear. Simultaneously she became conscious of an indecipherable stream, or streams, of thought passing through her head at hypersonic speed.

It was as if an industrial battery's worth of electricity was firing from synapse to synapse through her brain, electrons flushing through it as though it were a copper wire, dispersing frantically throughout, as if trying to find somewhere to hide. She felt as though she was going to pass out. Whatever this feeling was, it was taking over her whole body, each wave coming on faster and hitting harder than the last. She was definitely going to pass out. Her vision began to fade, narrowing vertically like rotated reinforced lift doors. Then, like the flick of a switch, pure darkness.

II. Goma Taki

A flipbook of frantic, blurred and incoherent visions appeared before the girl's eyes. In one instance a distorted image of a girl, not dissimilar in appearance to herself, flashed before her, the girl appearing clearly distressed and emotionally torn, as if stuck in an almighty battle of conscience. The image was quickly literally ripped in two, as if being pulled from each side by independent forces in dispute, revealing entirely new scenes, one after the other, in rapid fashion. Appearing and fading into the next far too quick to be made sense of, the images rolled and crashed into the next like the waves of a biblically stormy ocean. The only constant was a girl, presumably the same girl throughout, appearing to be the focal point of some sort of freakish nightmare. The girl experienced all of this in what seemed like an instant, she felt as though her body was thrashing about, trying to escape the powerful visions. Abruptly the girl's consciousness was thrust forward, launched from her own body into the body of the girl in the visions. She now found herself in the body of the girl, tied down, strapped by the wrists, ankles and neck by rough leather straps to a bed in the middle of a dimly lit room. Time slowed briefly, allowing the girl to feel every bit of overwhelming fear surging through her body and mind, if only for a moment, before the girl's conscience was thrust back into her own body to the distant sound of clicking.

Click Click... Click Click Click! The girl awoke gradually to the presence of Libi, caringly knelt down by the side of her, snapping her fingers in front of her face in an effort to wake her. Libi sensed that the girl was regaining consciousness. She smiled, and placed her warm hand gently on top of the girl's.

"How are you feeling?" she asked the girl, with a sincere concern for the girl's wellness.

The girl felt too weak and dazed to answer. She was still coming around, simultaneously adjusting to the feeling of being back inside her own body again and trying to make sense of her surroundings.

"We moved you back in here thinking you might be more comfortable here for now," Libi explained. The girl was able to prop herself up slightly onto her elbows. As she did so she recognised the texture of the antique woollen rug beneath her. She was back in the front room of the house, the one she had woken up in just a couple of hours earlier. A quick glance right and left confirmed her suspicions, yep, she was right back where she had started this dreamlike experience, facing the exact same direction. Even the cat was sitting facing her, as it was the first time, staring at her with its piercing diamond-centred green eyes. As she glanced left she became startled by a figure, one she definitely did not recognise, bearing down over her. Faintly muddied grey Wellington boots on his feet led the girls gaze up to a pair of blue denim dungarees with shiny silver buckles and buttons. Behind this a brown and white chequered shirt. His face was friendly and disarming, just like the others; kind lips half covered by his bushy hair comb moustache, matching his dark brown eyebrows and short, messy grey-tinged hair. Minimal blotches of dirt and sweat scattered scantily upon his wrinkled and sun-kissed arms, hands and face. His vaguely musky scent corresponded to his workman-like appearance, and if it weren't for Libi's overbearingly sensational scent, it would have likely been the most prominent smell dispersing throughout the room. The man noted the girl's bewilderment at his presence, and sought to quash her uneasiness.

"I'm the gardener," his deep voice soothed the girl's on-edge nerves slightly. "I was just coming in for the evening when I saw you collapsed on the floor here. I noticed Libi was attending to you so knew you were in capable hands. Still, I wanted to make sure you were feeling okay when you came to," he explained. The comforting combination of the gardener's wholehearted words and the touch of Libi's warming supple skin upon her hand made her feel gradually at ease. It dawned on her in this moment that these people around her now were all she knew, all she had at this moment in time. Needless to say this was a scary realisation, yet it also gave her a feeling of immediate connection to them. They were being objectively nice to her, making her feel welcome, and she thought to herself that maybe this place, although still completely unexplained and senseless, wasn't so bad after all. Libi, the gardener and the girl exchanged polite smiles, the three of them almost breaking out into subdued giggles, this was the girl's way of reassuring them that she was okay.

"What the hell was that?" she asked vehemently, and semi-rhetorically.

"It seemed you didn't like your room too much, but I think you'll get used to it soon," Libi remarked.

"Haha yeah, I'm sure you will," the gardener added, with a chuckle.

"Seemed you had quite the nightmare there too," Libi followed up, with concern upon her face.

"Yeah it was pretty crazy," the girl replied. "Didn't make any sense," she added, attempting to demonstrate the bizarre and incoherent nature of the visions she had experienced with a bemused look on her face.

"Mhmm," Libi nodded, understandingly. Both Libi and the gardener appeared sympathetic but not overly concerned. It appeared as if they potentially had some sort of omniscient knowledge of what the girl had just experienced, or maybe they were just glad that she seemed okay. Either way, the girl however was too mentally and physically fatigued by the experience to even notice.

"You just missed dinner too, shame, the chef would have seen to the scraps by now. You have to be prompt in this house if you expect to be fed," the gardener followed up, again with a chuckle, reinforcing the jovial nature of his comment. He adjusted his posture and bent his elbows, resting his hands on his hips. The girl shifted her vision back across to her right. She could see through the small domed window in the front door that the sun was in the process of setting, making it likely early evening. 'How long was I out for?' she pondered to herself, perhaps too scared to ask the question out-loud to the others. Before she had the chance to reconsider this, in walked another figure from the doorway directly in front of her.

"How is she doing?" posed the figure, another man, shorter in stature than the others, very well dressed and well groomed. Shirt, tie, thin dark blue crew neck cotton jumper, expensive watch, smart grey trousers, smart black shoes, clean shaven, combover, the lot. He looked like an entrepreneur of sorts, sadly not a very good looking one. This however did not stop the girl having some feeling of attraction towards him, whether it was the cheesy white smile or simply his clearly well looked after appearance, or purely intrigue more than anything else. His face was tinged with an ignorant sense of failure or desperation, making him verging on endearing.

"Think she's okay now, just a bit shaken up still," Libi responded to the man.

"Understandably," the man declared, his presumably expensive cologne beginning to waft towards the girl. "Crazy dream right?" he too sympathised with the girl. The girl didn't reply and instead just stared at him. She felt as though she knew him, that she had met him before. But how could she have? She concluded internally that she just must have still been feeling odd from her traumatic episode.

"My name is," the man started to convey, however the girl abruptly interjected.

"Greed," she blurted out, appearing stunned at what had just happened. She knew this man's name, having never met him before, and then watched it escape her mouth, almost instinctively.

"That's right," said the man, "That's what the other's call me anyway," he added. He seemed somewhat appreciative that the girl knew his name. As the girl questioned how she had acquired this information, she came upon another bemusing realisation. She could now picture the layout of the rest of the house, she knew which rooms were where, even though she had not yet fully explored it. 'How is this possible?' she wondered to herself, completely dumbfounded by the new knowledge she now possessed. She could picture each room vaguely in her head, knowing which room led to the next, however she was unable to envisage exactly the contents of each room, this part was unclear to her. She remembered a third bedroom that she had not yet been to, an adequately stocked library, and even the layout of the farm and garden area, which again she had not yet been to. The library, she understood, was of inherent importance and value, though she did not know why. The sense of power and significance that the cold stone-walled library may hold scared her, and her apprehensions were so extensive that she decided to force this epiphany to the back of her mind for now. These powerful secrets were to be another day's treasure.

"Can you tell me who I am and what I'm doing here now?" the girl asked the others with renewed optimism.

Libi, Greed and the gardener all looked at each other in apparent disappointment. The gardener gently shook his head at the others. All three of them turned their heads back to look directly at the girl, in unsettlingly peculiar unison. To the girl the sincerely affectionate looks upon their facing seemed to nullify this eerie synchronisation.

"Not tonight, you need to rest, been an eventful day," the gardener stated, compassionately. "Just know that you're safe here," he added, reassuringly.

The girl, now propped up fully by her hands while still sitting on the densely woven rug, was not entirely happy with this response, however she was far too drained from the experience to argue. She concluded with herself that she would do some investigating of her own later on, without their knowledge, in the hope of figuring out what was truly going on here, once she felt more up to the task. She kept this plan to herself, obviously.

"We're all about to go and sit round the fire in the lounge, we'd love for you to join us," Libi asserted. She tenderly moved her hand from on top of the girl's and placed it suggestively onto the girl's outstretched leg, just above her knee. Even through the layer of denim separating their skin the girl could feel the affectionate warmth of Libi's elegant hand. The girl tried her hardest not to flinch in mild excitement.

"Okay," the girl replied, locking eyes with Libi, before looking up to the gardener and then Greed, smiling at them all in succession. Libi helped the girl to her feet and continued her assistance as the girl gingerly hobbled through the first archway, along the narrow corridor, and through the second archway to their right, into the lounge.

A fire was already invitingly roaring inside the fireplace, filling the room with a delightfully ambient glow. Upon the sofa remained the scruffy-ish looking man from earlier, appearing as though he had not moved an inch from when the girl last saw him. In front of the fireplace, the left-most two of the six seats were already filled, one by the chef and one by yet another completely unfamiliar looking character. An older lady, perhaps in her late forties or early fifties with a greying bob haircut and wire-framed reading glasses. She sat with immaculate posture, in an arguably pretentious manner, her half skirt half tight covered legs crossed, one over the other. The woman and the chef turned, again in eerily robotic unison, and smiled at the girl entering the room with the others. The girl stared at the unknown woman as she approached the fireplace. Libi encouraged the girl to sit on the stool next to the woman, the third seat along from the left in the crescent-shaped row of six. The girl sat down on the seat next to the woman, still trying to analyse her nature, but the woman did not outwardly give much away.

"It appears you don't remember me, but of course I remember you," the woman projected in a proud tone toward the girl. She had managed to read the girl's body language effectively. The girl, reluctant to be belittled, spoke calmly back;

"I'm afraid I don't, sorry," the girl replied, while desperately trying to forage her mind for any information at all about this woman. She felt the vaguest of recognition about the woman, at least by the aura she gave off if not in looks alone. The girl engaged in polite small talk with the lady, almost subconsciously, as she endeavoured to muster some recollection of the woman. It was coming to her, slowly, as their seemingly meaningless background conversation continued, the information was developing itself onto the tip of her tongue, it was now tantalisingly close, but it just wouldn't appear.

Had it not been for the massively helping hand of the waft of faint vanilla lignin paper and leather, it may have never presented itself. 'The library!' the girl's eureka moment finally materialised, in a flash.

"The library!" the girl interrupted their benign conversation in the same eureka-occurring breath. She appeared reservedly smug with herself at reaching this announcement.

"That's right," the woman responded.

"What's your name?" the girl asked in anticipation, contemplating for a moment if she was going to be able to remember all of these new names, in turn making her reflect on what a long and strange day she had up to this point.

"'How vain, without the merit, is the name'," the woman replied with an air of condescension. The girl looked at the woman blankly, expecting more.

"Homer," the woman added, reciprocating the girl's blank expression. After a pause of awkward silence the woman followed up;

"I'm joking, don't worry," she said cheerfully, cutting through the uncomfortable tension swiftly. "I'm the library-keeper, but you can call me what you want, as long as it's nice," she added again in a jovial manner. Like the others the woman emanated a sociable friendliness, and once the girl gave in to engaging in significant conversation with the woman, she found her to be similarly charming and welcoming. Before long, all six of them were deep in amiable conversations, glowing in amber warmth and light, sitting around the fire. With the help of a mug of hot chocolate (the chef's own especially decadent recipe), the girl's inhabitations were quickly discarded by the warming spirit of the people and the fireplace in combination, and she became quickly lost to the conversations. A significant amount of time passed before the girl's conscience would break from behind this veil of sanctuary. At this point the sky outside was merely a deep bluey-black canvas for the scattered pin-prick stars, as evenly displayed as the girl had ever seen. Such a darkness in the sky prompted, surely, for a closing of the curtains, yet this task was never enacted, for whatever reason. The scene looked and felt somewhat primal, a family sat around a blazing fire under the stars of the dark night sky telling stories passed down for generations. Perhaps this is why the girl felt so at home in the situation. Furthermore, this was of course the predominant method through which all human knowledge was shared and developed, for thousands of years. The content of the conversations did not seem obviously useful nor directly applicable to the girl's current situation, but regardless, there was a distinct possibility that the girl, whether consciously or not, was using this as an opportunity to learn. A few jovial ghost stories and urban myths interspersed among casual anecdotal tales from each of them developed into the more thought-provoking topics of theology, mythology and ethics. The girl listened intently as each of the characters sat around her began to develop and she gained a better understanding of each. After a couple of hours' worth of conversation, the girl had managed to build a mental notebook of assumptions about them all:

- Libi – constantly endearing, warm and honest. A yet undiscovered passion and desire surrounded them when they spoke.
- The gardener – gentle, soft-hearted and the best story-teller. Possibility of having a darker, angrier side to him.
- The chef – lovable, full of life and accommodating, yet slightly secretive and insecure.
- Greed – innocent but mildly attention-seeking, seemed somewhat of an outsider to the group. The true reason behind his name is still not understood.
- The library-keeper – had a pretentious and somewhat condescending front that easily dissolved to reveal a compassionate motherly figure, eager to teach and share knowledge

The accuracy of said assumptions was of course down to the accuracy of her judgement, which to this point the girl had no reason to distrust. Although now she considered it, she also had no real reason to trust it either.

It was at one moment later on in the evening, seemingly an innocuous a moment as any other so far, as the entertaining conversations and story-telling continued around her, that the girl's attention seemed to be gradually pulled towards the heart of the fire. Inside the white smooth stone fireplace, solid circular oak wood logs sat piled upon each other, with the centre of the pile glowing deep crimson red like the magma core of the earth. Now fully focused on the relentless power of the epicentre of the flames, reflecting perfectly in her honest blue eyes, the girl entered a trance-like state. She could feel the fire beckoning to her mind, craving every last bit of her attention, drawing her in. She did not feel scared, nor intimidated, nor excited for that matter. She felt nothing. The flames grew bigger and more intense right in front of her, expanding to fill her entire field of vision. Imagine a dollhouse version of Satan's Lair – that is what she is staring into; and the doors had just flung open. She experienced a brief respite from the intensity of the flame to her eyes as a concealed, boarded up wall behind the shimmering white stone of the fireplace made itself visible to her. It was as though the girl was given the temporary superpower of x-ray vision. In an instant she recognised it, she now remembered there was another room in the house, boarded up and hidden behind the wall in which the fireplace was sunken. With this realisation, the girl was partially removed from her trance, however her focus was still on the fire. She began to distinguish what looked like small paper notes, thin brittle pieces of paper with gracefully hand-written texts on them, deep in the fire. She focused on one piece of the charred tea-stained pieces of paper and to her amazement it appeared as though the text was still being written onto it. Before her very eyes the black quill-tip written text was being frantically written upon the paper, or so it seemed. As soon as the text came to an end with a definitive full stop, the piece of paper ignited at once and in a small flash of bright light it was completely incinerated. Precisely as this happened, the others around her broke out into a joint raucous of a laugh. Although the laughs were objectively harmless and were a consistent theme of the whole night, this time it made the girl feel differently, to her ears the sound was edged with a sinister undertone. With the backdrop of the gradually deepening, softening and increasingly disturbing cackles ringing in her ears, the girl noticed an object deep within the flames, balanced upon the burning logs. At first it was extremely indiscernible, a hazy, black… thing, a black core with blurred fuzzy edges. As the object became clearer the girl's expression turned from curious to horrified. She let out a piercing involuntary scream at the top of her lungs. The object that had gradually come into focus from the satanic flames was a black and white cat – *the* cat – helplessly trapped inside the fire like some sort of sick ritualistic effigy. The others noted her discomfort at once, all turning to her in support.

"It's okay," said Libi, again taking her hand comfortingly. Once more it was as if she knew what the girl had just witnessed. Even faster than the image of the cat had appeared, it disappeared, and with it the real, living cat jumped to the girl's aid out of nowhere and rubbed itself up between the girl's legs affectionately, as if it too were trying to say 'It's okay'.

"You must be exhausted, perhaps it's best you try and get some rest," stated the gardener. The others nodded in agreement. Still visibly shaken, the girl complied. Not only was the girl too exhausted from the relentlessly senseless nature of the day to resist, she also thought to herself that an opportunity to explore the house further and investigate alone may well present itself if everyone else followed suit and went to their separate rooms to rest. She followed Libi, who offered to escort the girl to her room, where she could rest. As she rose to her feet she peered up inquisitively at the clock above the fireplace, noticing that both arms had not moved at all, both ornate black metal tips still glued precisely to 'XII'. This reminded her of the man lying on the sofa, who had told her about the uselessness of the clocks in the house. Walking steadily toward the archway to exit the room, she looked back over her left shoulder at the sloth-like figure, still laid upon the high-backed antique sofa, motionless but for the gentle rolling rhythm of his chest moving up and down in breath. Still appearing as though he had not moved an inch throughout the whole evening, laying arms crossed and eyes closed on his back, the girl thought to herself: 'How on earth am I supposed to get any sleep with this creep in the house?'. She reminded herself that sleep was not the most important item on the agenda, and that she instead was going to endeavour to find out what was actually going on here and how, or if, she could escape, whilst the others rested. Besides, she could not see the lazily immobile man being of much hindrance to her.

It wasn't until the girl, under Libi's guidance, had begun to approach the door to her room from the bland square-shaped hallway room prior to it that she remembered what had happened earlier when she entered her room the first time. A new, formidable wave of anxiety arose inside her body, consuming her from the tip of her toes swiftly up to the hairs on her head. She slowed to a nervous halt half way through the hallway room, the undeniably soft carpet beneath her bare feet offering little solace to her fretful state of mind. Her palms began to weep sweat, particularly the palms, making them slimy to the touch. Her toes and fingers began to curl, her fingers eventually locking into a fist and her uniform toenails scratching and digging into the surface of the carpet slightly. This room and the approach to her bedroom door, made the house seem more disturbingly silent than anywhere else in the house. Was it going to happen again? Was she going to faint again? The girl's panic was intensifying, the room in front of her, even though still with the door to it firmly closed, giving her the same overwhelming fear as before.

"It's okay, it will be okay this time, I promise," reassured Libi, having noticed the girl's obvious discomfort and panicked body language. Every time Libi spoke, it meant something to the girl, she really did have a way of making her feel better, without fail. The overwhelming scale of her anxiety however could only be partly quashed by Libi's comforting and understanding presence. Attempting to do whatever she could to calm herself down, the girl thought up an idea to focus entirely on the door in front of her in all its detail, in order to remove her mind from her limitlessly creepy surroundings and apprehensions about the room which it concealed. Unfortunately there was not much detail to perceive about the door, it was a relatively basic, wooden door painted (immaculately, to be fair) creamy-white. She noticed that the pattern created by chiselled detailing on the door separated the upper portion of it into four panelled sections, surrounded by a semi-thick rectangular outer border. Although all part of the same singular piece of wood, the chiselled grooves presented the shallow projection of a cruciform cross, highlighted by the rudimentary shadowing of the grooved wood created from the light above the girl's head. This was enough detail at least for the girl to focus on, calming her nerves to a more sustainable level. Libi prompted the girl to open the door to the room, with a reassuring hand on her back. The magical tingling warmth of Libi's palm and fingers managed to sink through the girl's thin blouse top and onto her skin, as though the thin cotton was not even there. The combination of emotions the girl was experiencing, and had experienced cumulatively throughout the day, were becoming overbearing, and she now became eager to spend some time alone. With this, she mustered the courage, with Libi's reassuring words at the forefront of her mind, to lunge forward, grab the cold metal handle and fling the door wide open, taking a small step back in apprehension immediately as she did so. Her body and mind reacted similarly to the room as it did earlier. Her anxiety grew, she sensed something profound, whether good or evil, about the room. Although her discomfort continued to grow, it did not hit her quite in the same way it did the first time. It was more manageable, and the girl was able to rationalise the ever-growing anxiety consuming her body yet again. Fighting the constant fear urging her to turn and run for her life, the girl edged closer to the room. By the time she reached the innocuously luke-warm doorway to the room she was so emotionally drained that it was all-consuming. Finally, the girl let go of her anxiety and apprehension, giving in to whatever fate of hers the room may hold. She collapsed to the floor, only preventing her face and abdomen from crashing into the beige carpeted hard floor with her hands and knees. As she sat in a crumpled heap on the floor, visions ventured to flood her mind yet again, some echoing those of before, and some completely new yet inherently related. Once again the visions, even more incoherent and blurred than before, came to an abrupt end with the girl finding herself strapped down to a bed in a dimly-lit room, frightened for her life. In the background she could hear the ever-so-faint stomp of heavy boots, edging ever-closer, in tandem with it a sinister chuckle. Cutting the vision abruptly short, the girl's consciousness was thrust without warning back into her physical body by the nurturing grasp of Libi's arms around her shoulders. Appearing clearly sympathetic and concerned for the girl, Libi helped her from her heap up and onto the bed in the middle of the room.

As Libi lovingly wished her goodnight and encouraged her to rest, kissed her forehead gently and held her hand for a second or two, the girl lay atop the covers of the bed almost paralysed, staring gauntly at the blank ceiling of the room. Without any response from the girl Libi switched off the bedside lamp and exited the room, closing the door behind her, leaving the girl in complete and utter darkness. Even though she was completely exhausted she could not sleep, no matter how hard she tried. Understandably this could just be down to the bizarre and unsettling circumstances in which she found herself. With barely a twitch of movement throughout, the girl lay there for what could have been five minutes, or could have equally been two hours. Either way, it was just enough time for her brain and body to recover enough for her to consider her plan of action.

She fumbled around trying to find the switch to the bedside lamp to her right, eventually but not without struggling to find it and flicking on the light. It barely lit the room, mostly just providing a gloomy orange light over the girl and her bed which in turn looked like a small circular illuminated platform above a black abyss. She sat up slightly with her back leant against propped up pillows, as much as the stumpy raw wood headframe would allow. Although she attempted to resist this fact, the girl knew that the library was important, potentially crucial, and therefore after a short amount of deliberation she reluctantly decided that this had to be the first place she would visit in the search for information. The girl was able to encourage herself up off of the bed and she crept towards the door as light-footed as possible, so as to not inform anyone of her movement. With each delicate tip-toe she tried harder to not make a sound, to the point where by the time she had reached the door her toes were throbbing. She eked open the door as quietly as possible, only opening it just enough for her to squeeze her slim figure through sideways. She recalled from one of her dream-like visions that the inside of the library was made from stone bricks, like that of a mediaeval castle, and she therefore inferred that this must have been inside of the clunky metal doorway surrounded by the mediaeval-looking stone wall that was behind her when she first awoke in the front room. So that is where she headed. The girl continued in her efforts to be as quiet as humanly possible, past Libi's room and through the corridor, deciding to take a slightly more flat-footed approach as her toes succumbed to unsustainable agony. She noticed throughout her journey the intensely silent nature of the house, but tried to perceive this as a positive, as it likely meant all of the others would be sleeping. As she approached the archway in the left of the corridor that led to the lounge she noticed that the fire must have been on its mere last remaining embers as only a trail of dull red glow could now be seen emanating from it. She stealthily peered around the side of the archway and with great relief the only person to be seen was the unkempt idle man, whom the girl seemed to have a greater disliking for every time she saw him, remaining laid upon the sofa as he was before. Fuelled by her giddying sense of relief, the girl made it right to the end of the corridor and to the archway that led to the front room, at a marginally faster pace. As she made the journey down the corridor she appeared to be contemplating her decision, her mind was clearly fraught with indecision, like she was trying to convince herself of a way out of going to the library.

'What if I'm not ready for what is to be discovered there?' she thought to herself nervously. She concluded to herself: 'The quicker I find out what's going on here the quicker I can leave, and the library is currently the best hope I have at finding this out.'. As if it were a wish pleaded for by her subconscious mind and granted to her by this ever-unpredictable house, the final decision was made for her. Upon reaching the archway to the front room, she noticed that the bulky wooden front door of the house was wide open. She expected a change of temperature, perhaps at least a mild breeze or chill from the outside air, but no, the room had kept at the perfect temperature, as had the entirety of the house. The girl had a quick glance at the kitchen door, which was closed shut, and then proceeded to approach the open door to her left, keeping up her attempts to remain silent. It had not taken much at all for the girl to seemingly forget all about her decidedly sensible plan to make the library her first port of call. She stepped through the front door and to her mild surprise the evening air felt just as pleasantly lukewarm as it had in the daytime. The gravel beneath her feet felt identical in temperature and in mildly jagged texture. In fact, at first glance, the entirety of her surroundings felt and looked the same. It was as if someone had simply switched out a light from the daytime, with everything else having remained the same. The girl surveyed the scene, looking to her left she saw the identical gravel path leading around to little but a few bushes and trees, in front of her the edge of this 'island' she found herself on. On seeing the island edge again it made the girl rethink just how bizarre and unexplained this situation was, and as she cautiously peered over the edge of the land she thought back to the awful sinking feeling in her stomach she had experienced earlier that day when she realised that she had no clue who she even was, let alone where she was. It was hard for the girl not to feel sorry for herself, complete sorrow came over her, she felt completely lost, alone and terrified. She felt like collapsing in a sorry heap on the floor again, in resignation, but managed to distract herself by continuing her inspection of her surroundings. Looking to her right the girl noticed something different, something stood out to her that did not stand out earlier on in the day. Through the narrow gaps in the wooden panels, frayed with tiny splinters, of the small farmer-style hut over by the crop-growing farm area the girl could see an ambient fluorescent yellow-green glow. The glow was intense but small, in the sense that whatever was emitting it would have fit in the palms of the girl's hands. It was low to the floor, suggesting whatever it was had been placed on the floor, for now at least. Out of the corner of her eye she noticed another glowing object, smaller, like a firefly, yet with the exact same fluorescent glow about it. This time it was moving, slowly but surely towards the farmers hut from the back right corner of the farm area. The girl squinted, trying to get a better view of the flying object, and as she did, she began to hear a *clump, clump* noise. The noise continued, echoing slightly in the empty dark night sky, until the glowing object reached the farmers hut, at which point the door was opened with a subtle creaking of its rudimentary brass hinges, and the girl realised that the noise she could hear was the now unmistakable sound of the gardener's wellington boots traversing across the grass-topped firm muddy ground. He was clearly harvesting something, a fruit or vegetable that the girl had not seen before perhaps. But at this hour of the night? The girl, somewhat dumbfounded by this, stood still and patiently contemplated her next move. 'Should I go and see what the gardener is collecting?' she questioned to herself, 'He was friendly enough earlier, no need to be scared of him, right?' she thought. In this moment of contemplation she also remembered her original plan for the evening – to visit the library. Caught in yet another moment of indecision, the girl stood silently for a short while, an invisible damp fog weighing down slightly on her shoulders as if to stress the importance of the decision to be made.

Ding-a-ling! Ding-a-ling-a-ling! The girl launched herself into the air in shock as the piercing noise of a bell rang multiple times down by her feet. It was the cat! The girl was not even aware up to this point that the cat wore a bell on its collar, or that it even had a collar! But there it was, sitting unwittingly at the girl's feet, expressionless, having just alerted the gardener as to her whereabouts. Having looked down at the cat for merely a second or two, the girl heard the sound of the gardener's wellington boots again, this time getting closer and closer, louder and louder, and at a much more purposeful pace. The girl instinctually looked up in the direction of the farmers hut. To add to her shock and intensifying panic, the gardener was already halfway between the hut and the girl, and was wielding a green metal-tipped pitchfork.

'Shit!' thought the girl to herself, now panic-stricken and completely unsure of what to do. Her immense fear glued her to the spot, she was a sitting duck.

III. Azrael

Within a few frantic short breaths the gardener came to a halt just a couple of paces away from the girl. Both of their faces were dimly lit by the few metal lanterns on the floor that highlighted the edge of the gravel path and the front door to the house. The gardener bent down, crouching his knees and swooped up one of the black lanterns that resembled that of a coal mine, each emitting a hazy orange glow. He stood back to his feet, all in one smooth motion, and held the lantern up by its swinging handle, between his and the girl's faces. The girl, still standing frozen to the spot, her muscles as rigid as ever, couldn't tell if he was angry, or what he was about to do next.

"What are you doing out here?" the gardener asked, seeming more concerned than angry, although the girl was still nervous and unsure. "You're supposed to be resting," he added, with a more conclusively concerned look coming across his face.

"S-sorry," the girl stuttered, her body beginning to gradually warm up from the shock of the situation. "I couldn't sleep so I went for a walk around the house, and then I noticed the front door was open," the girl added, apologetically. Her mind was matching her body in slowly coming back to clarity, like she was waking up from a bad dream.

"Ah that was my fault, I must have left the door open. You really should try and get some rest though," the gardener insisted, clearly showing compassion toward the girl. The girl was in no mood to argue, and therefore allowed the gardener to show her back to her room, where she could regroup her emotions and decide what to do next. It appeared as though everyone in the house had somehow been notified of her night-time wander. Each of the house members stood to attention outside their respective rooms and watched with care as the girl passed, most without making a sound. In the front room, in front of the stone brick wall and mediaeval-looking metal door stood the library-keeper, arms crossed and mild concern across her face, while the chef stood in the doorway to the kitchen, his plump stature almost filling it entirely. Both of them followed the girl with their eyes from the front door into the corridor to the right without saying a word. It was unsettlingly creepy, yet the girl seemed still too exhausted to appreciate the full extent of this. They walked back down the corridor, passed the now completely dark lounge with the fire now entirely extinguished, and through the square shaped room in which stood Libi and Greed. Greed, stood by the archway to another corridor to the right of the room, was acting very similarly to the library-keeper and chef in the front room, and it was only Libi, stood at the entrance to her room, that broke the growingly unbearable silence, holding out her hand palm up as an offering of comfort to the girl.

"Are you okay?" Libi asked, clearly distressed with concern for the girl.

"Yeah, I just couldn't sleep," the girl responded timidly.

"If you can't sleep, maybe try this," said Libi, handing the girl a small black ceramic pot with ten to twenty thin sticks sticking out of it, and a small box of matches. The sticks were covered in a dark greeny-black substance that was hardened. The girl accepted the gifts with open hands, partly as she felt too shy to do anything else, and as she did so a soothing dark and herbaceous musky scent wafted past the girl like a enveloping gust of wind. Immediately the smell took hold of the girl, making her extremities tingle and her brain go slightly numb. She assumed that whatever Libi had given her she had been using herself in her room and had caused this nauseatingly consuming scent. Thankfully at this range the potency of which was bearable, and so the girl gratefully took the gifts and walked on towards her room.

"Thanks," she uttered awkwardly, pretending to ignore the effects of the scent emerging from Libi's room.

"If you still can't sleep, you can always come and sleep with me in here," Libi promptly suggested, hesitantly and eagerly awaiting the girl's response.

"Okay, thanks," the girl responded, not even looking up from the floor as she now faced away from Libi, heading toward her bedroom, with the gardener still supporting in tow. At the doorway to her room the gardener and Libi bid the girl another goodnight, while Greed remained silent, all of them watching with concern as the girl entered her bedroom. All of them followed the girl intently in unison with their eyes eerily, until the girl had wearily closed the door behind her. The girl proceeded to lie back down in bed, putting the gifts she had received from Libi aside on the bedside table, without giving them much thought at all. She lay flat on her back, staring mindlessly at the ceiling of the room under the ambient glow of the bedside lamp for a short while, exhausted. She began reasoning with herself that surely this must just be an extremely weird and convoluted dream she was having, and that all she needed to do to escape it was wake herself up. She was however unconvinced by this theory as she wondered how it would be possible that she would be feeling such strong physical sensations while in a dream as she had since being there. She thought back to the paresthesia in her legs and feet when she first awoke in the front room, then the various waves of anxiety and fear that had come across her body at numerous times of the day, which on one occasion even caused her to pass out. Surely this was not possible inside a dream? Her mind fluttered back and forth pondering over her theory, what else could it be other than just a truly fucked up dream?

Unable to reach a solid conclusion, the girl decided to turn her mental efforts towards thinking about what she should do next. How could she wake herself up if it was just a dream? She abruptly drew the fingers of her right hand toward her left arm and pinched hard in frustration, her nails just long enough to send a mild sharp pain shooting up her left arm. Nothing. Again with no conclusive answer to her quandaries she decided it best she tried to do some more investigating before taking more decisive action. She remembered that there were still more rooms of the house to explore, including the boarded-up hidden room located somewhere behind the lounge. Presumably from her earlier episode of unconsciousness and resulting delirious visions, she believed that she could recall a second entrance to the boarded-up room, located in the bathroom. The girl decided it best to leave it a while before leaving her room again, to give everyone a chance to settle back in their own rooms, and also to allow for the girl to once again recover enough energy for the task. Again unable to sleep, the girl waited a sufficient amount of time, or at least until she couldn't bear the mind-numbing silence and lack of stimulation anymore, before carefully getting out of bed and to her feet. She mirrored her movements from earlier in the night almost to a tee, quietly and cautiously traversing the bedroom floor. Upon reaching the door, she pried it open perhaps even more carefully than the first time, half expecting someone to be waiting for her on the other side. Instead all she could see was pure darkness. Still wary that there could be someone, or something, waiting for her in the room, she painstakingly felt her away out through the bedroom doorway and along the left wall, knowing that if she followed this round for long enough she would reach the other corridor, which she believed led to Greed's room and more importantly the bathroom. Without the discouragement of any noise coming from anywhere but the gentle sound of her soft fingertips gliding along the orange-peel textured walls and the occasional squeak of a floorboard beneath her trepidatious footsteps, the girl was able to navigate the room as intended by following the rout of the left hand wall, which had one perpendicular change of direction to the right before guiding her to what she hoped was the archway to the other corridor. Taking her first step through the archway, still in complete darkness, she was still entirely unsure if she was heading the right way, as beneath her feet was a replica of the delightfully springy carpet that also covered the floor of the other corridor. However, barring a wildly inaccurate calculation of direction, the girl concluded to herself that she must be heading the right way. Ten or so footsteps into her journey down the corridor, she noticed the faintest of lights leaking from an extra thin rectangular shaped crevice, highlighting the outline of what must surely be a door. The girl deciphered that to her left must be the archway to the second box-shaped room, which led on to Greed's room in the back right corner (all of this resulting from her unexplained seemingly inherent memory of the layout of the house that she had been gifted with earlier in the day), which is where she could see the faint outline of his bedroom door being created by a weak lightsource within his room. 'Does this mean that he is awake?' the girl thought to herself with worry. Before she could even begin to contemplate her next move, she heard a considerably quiet 'Meow... meow,' coming from somewhere over by Greed's door. 'Not again,' the girl thought to herself with mild frustration. 'That bloody cat'. Deciding it would be foolish to try and make a quick dash for the end of the corridor toward the bathroom, the girl instead gently crept over to the intermittent sound of the cat.

'Meow... meow'. The sound echoed gently in the noiseless room. 'Is it getting louder or am i just getting closer?' the girl pondered, her panic growing slightly. As she got closer to the sound she felt around somewhat frantically with her hands in order to try and locate the cat and pet it into silence. For a few desperate moments the girl felt around with her hands in all directions while crouched as low as she could get to her floor, now positioned only a few steps from Greed's bedroom door. As if it had had enough of toying with the girl, the cat took a few silent pawsteps closer to the girl and sat back beside her left leg as the girl finally felt its silken fur. The girl sighed in relief, stroking the cat gently with both hands. The girl took refuge in this calming moment, and some of her anxiety-laden emotions began secreting into the velvety soft black and white fur of the cat. She was not afforded much time at all before the girl was thrust backward onto her bottom as the door in her now close proximity to her right opened, startled by both the pure unexpectedness of Greed opening his door and the deceiving brightness of the light emanating from his now visible room.

"Hey," Greed spoke, disarmingly softly. The girl immediately recalled her instinctual fondness of Greed, and her shock quickly diluted.

"Hi," she said back, hesitantly and without yet getting back to her feet.

"The boarded-up room is a waste of time, trust me," Greed advised. The kind innocent smile upon his face never seemed to leave.

"How did you know I was going there?" the girl questioned, once again dumbfounded. She simultaneously clambered back to her feet and brushed her hands together to sweep off a few collected cat hairs.

"Just trust me, waste of time," Greed responded, adamantly. He appeared somewhat frustrated that he could not tell the girl more, no matter how much he wanted to. Each of his hands were resting at just below shoulder height on the doorframe to his bedroom, slightly like he was guarding the entrance. Past his silhouette the girl could see into his room behind him, and at once one of her so far unanswered mysteries was explained. Greed's room was stacked full of miscellaneous ornaments, furniture and other pieces of decoration. 'That's why the rest of the house is so bare,' the girl thought to herself, finding it a somewhat humorous revelation. 'And that's why the others call him Greed,' she thought, again seeing the humour in the situation. She looked back up at Greed, who stood in the doorway protectively and looked rather embarrassed. The girl felt immediate empathy for Greed.

"I'm sorry if I woke you," she stated, attempting to come across friendly in order to quash Greed's apparent embarrassment.

"No it's okay, you didn't," Greed responded, still smiling, but still clearly somewhat embarrassed. The girl noticed that behind him, some on the back wall in his room and some piled among the other unholy amount of crap, were five-or-so clocks of varying styles, all with their hands not moving and stuck on twelve. This forced her to remember again the strange man who had been laid upon the sofa all day and all evening, and confirmed his earlier statement to her. 'The clocks don't work... They don't work, none of them do, never have,' she envisaged the conversation with the man, muttering to her in his idle state on the sofa. With a paradoxical trust in Greed to not tell the others yet a distrust in him having told her the full truth, the girl explained to Greed that she was still going to go and look at the boarded-up room for herself.

"Well okay, but I'm telling you it's not worth it,' Greed proceeded to respond with an air of resignation. "Goodnight, come and get me if you need anything," he added.

"Thanks, will do," replied the girl, before Greed seemingly hurried to close his door and escape the slightly awkward-turning encounter. Feeling as brave as ever up to this point, the girl felt her way back to the archway to the corridor and turned left, walking the full length of the corridor and reaching another door frame. This time the door was open, and the girl leant in through it and scrambled her hands about trying to find the cord for the lightswitch, which she instinctually knew was to her left. It didn't take long for her to find the long dangling cord, pulling it with an eager force.

Bam! The light turned on, violently spraying bright white light across the shiny surfaces of the bathroom floor and walls and out into the corridor. With a brief moment of realisation and panic, the girl instinctually jumped bolted through the doorway into the bathroom and closed the door behind her, perhaps a little too brutishly for her stealthy endeavours. The bright light, which appeared to be the most striking yet, took a little while for the girl's eyes to adjust to. She stood in the centre of the square-shaped bathroom, spinning around slowly trying to assess her surroundings as her vision regained clarity. She was thankful, at least, that the room she was in was indeed the bathroom. Furthermore, she was thankful that she was the only one in it, or so she could see. Before her vision had fully returned she noticed the slick tiled floor beneath her feet. The square-inch blue tiles were notably cold but were quickly warmed by the soles of her feet, evolving from bitterly chilled to warm in seconds. A similar style of tiling crept halfway up the walls, this time white in colour. While being sparkly clean and having a rather pleasant and homely feel to it, the bathroom was somewhat unremarkable. A proud white Victorian-style ceramic bathtub was the centrepiece, sat upon four black curved metal feet on the right hand side wall. Opposite this on the left wall was a grand mirror, spanning a full arm span flat against the wall, above a wide Victorian-style sink, perhaps twice as wide as what would be expected, with spotlessly shiny metal taps. The room seemed to be an attractive mix of Victorian-era and modern-style bathroom. Above the girl's head hung a mildly extravagant miniature brass chandelier, of which the girl pondered how Greed had not yet got his hands on, or why. Undeterred due to the unremarkable appearance of the bathroom, the girl's focus turned unhesitantly to finding the boarded-up room. It did not take her long at all to notice that in the wall behind the bath there was a painted-over outline of a door which had been boarded up with two panels of wood positioned diagonally in front of it, forming a

'X' shape, as if to say 'DO NOT ENTER'. 'Well that wasn't very hard,' the girl thought to herself, relieved but also slightly disappointed – she was evidently in the mood for a challenge. This disappointment was soon scuppered however as she realised the true challenge – how was she going to move the bath enough to get to the doorway, and then break through the barrier to the doorway and open the door all without making enough noise to alert anyone to her activities. Her concern over the matter rapidly turned to distress as she heard the ominous echo of footsteps approaching from the corridor. 'Shit!' the girl outwardly began to panic, searching for somewhere to hide before conceding and instead searching her mind for an excuse as to what she was doing. A few frenzied moments ensued, with the reverberating deep sound of the footsteps getting ever-closer and more daunting. They became like intimidating claps of thunder on a stormy night, growing in intensity. 'I'm allowed to go to the bathroom,' the girl thought, trying to calm herself as much as she possibly could. Her nerves, not even half settled by this thought grew to a climax as she stood as still as possible, holding her breath even, in the centre of the bathroom, staring intently at the door handle, expecting it to turn any moment.

Her nerves were not helped by the abrupt nature of the termination of the footsteps the moment they reached the bathroom door, the alarming thuds of which came to an instantaneously halt at the same time as it felt as though the girl's heart had stopped. For an unbearably eternal-feeling couple of seconds there was complete silence, causing a dizzying ringing in the girl's ears to build while the tiles beneath her feet regained their chilling temperature as all of the heat was seemingly sucked up through the girl's body and spread throughout, and her fingers and hands now completely numb. To her unfathomably immense relief and without even the sound of a turn or change of direction, the footsteps resumed but were now distinctly softening and distancing themselves from the bathroom door. The girl had to take a moment and sat on the toilet next to the sink, out of breath, the room spinning around her vision, her sweaty palms resting on her knees. She couldn't understand why she felt so panicked in that situation as no one she had so far met had given her any cause for concern, however she ultimately had to allow herself some leeway as she was experiencing a truly ridiculous combination of circumstances.

Now utterly exhausted and emotionally beaten, the girl again considered the bizarre nature of her situation. 'Surely this is just a dream, it has to be,' she thought to herself, this time a lot more assertively. Composing herself a bit more, she reluctantly conceded to the acknowledgment that she would not be able to get into the boarded-up room quietly enough to do it right now, no matter how important it may be. With this she decided to head back to her room, turning the light off behind her and sneaking as quietly as possible in her frail state, hoping that if she really tried she would be able to fall asleep in her bed and would wake up somewhere else, somewhere she remembered.

After an hour or two of restless tossing and turning, with endless thoughts running through her head, the girl's frustrations were growing. No matter how hard she tried she could not sleep. She eventually surrendered to her restless state and for another hour or so simply laid, again on her back, on the bed staring into the dark void above her. Somehow she managed to suppress her thoughts enough to relax, and for a short while she enjoyed a restful state upon her bed. Although it was impossible to tell, thanks to the wonderfully effective black-out curtains fixed at the fore of the window, the girl believed it must surely be morning by now. Nevertheless, she waited patiently for a short while, her weary state partially nourished by a couple of hours of mindless activity. Feeling as though she would not be able to get any more useful rest this evening, or morning, whatever it might be, the girl eventually grew impatient, sitting up and tuning on the bedside lamp. As she turned on the lamp, the light from it shined down onto the bedside table, upon which sat the curved-edged ceramic pot with the coated thin wooden sticks sticking out. The girl had forgotten all about this gift from Libi, having not taken much notice of it in the first place, which she instructed her to use if she continued to struggle to sleep. Somewhat annoyed with herself, the girl's frustrations worsened, before she noticed her bedroom door gently creep open. Sunlight pierced through the darkness of her room around the edges of the door, the amount of which steadily increased at a rate at which the girl could pleasantly acclimate. Once the door was two-thirds opened Libi's beautiful head came into full view as she peered into the room checking on the girl's status. She could see that the girl was sitting upright against the headboard of the bed and so took one step into the room, her phenomenal scent following, and reaching the girl in one wind-like gust.

"Good morning, did you manage to rest at all?" Libi asked, hoping for a positive response.

"Not really, but I feel a little bit better," replied the girl, drowsily.

"Ah well at least that's something," Libi responded back, positively. The girl still felt extremely tired and frustrated by her lack of knowledge, and was not at all interested in conversing with Libi, despite her friendly attitude and her spectacularly alluring scent. She therefore remained quiet, looking around her room, in the hope that Libi would leave.

"Well I'll leave you to it, let me know if you need anything," said Libi, as if she had read the girl's mind. She was being so nice that the girl found it bordering on annoying. Libi left without a response from the girl, only closing the door about half way, leaving it roughly one-third open. 'At least I know it's morning now,' the girl attempted to improve her own mood even marginally. She leaned back full against the headboard, her head against the wall, her neck angled up toward the ceiling, and sighed. After a short pause for thought, she thrust herself into action. 'Right, this is just a bad dream," she reminded herself of the previous night's conclusions as she hopped up from the bed and over to the curtains, flinging them open with a renewed sense of optimism. She looked out of the window, again partially enamoured by the sight of the tempting-looking fruit laden tree outside of it, stealing her gaze for another short while.

"Concentrate," she spoke sternly to herself out loud as the distraction of the snake-skin barked tree wore off. 'Right, one quick visit to the library to see if we can find out what is truly going on here, and if not then... well... I'm just going to have to wake myself up from this hellish dream!' her internal dialogue was growing in anger, matching the frustration in her facial expression and her sharp body movements and she stomped back and forth between the bed and the window. Then she turned and headed for the door, marched down through the hallway room and the corridor, ignoring everything else to either side of her, and into the front room. With a look of determination across her face, she headed towards the castle-style curved stone wall and metal door across from her. As she walked, she had a quick glance to her right into the kitchen, the door to which was wide open, and saw the chef, standing slicing vegetables in the exact same manner he was yesterday. This oddity only further enflamed the girl's frustrations, and her footsteps grew into minor stomps as she approached the metal door. Upon reaching the door, the girl calmed herself slightly, and without any further consideration grasped the right hand side of the door, prying it open with her finger tips. The door was very heavy, yet opened considerably easier than the girl was expecting, presumably thanks to well-oiled hinges, with the door swinging open slowly with its own weight after the girl's initial efforts. Instantly the girl was hit with the faint vanilla and leathery smell of books, the same aroma she had experienced yesterday evening after meeting the library-keeper. It was quite an enticing scent, and although the library was relatively dark, only lit by a few thin long white dripping candles and an extravagant domed shaped stained glass window that was in fact the entirety of the ceiling, the room felt comforting. The girl took a step up onto the slightly cold and damp feeling large stones making up the floor, matching the walls. She hoisted herself up the chunky stone step with her arms leveraging her weight on the stone brick door frame, her fingerprints and fingernails collecting a minute amount of sand-textured residue from the stone bricks. Starting to the left of her and spiralling up a narrow stone beam right in the centre of the library the girl observed a spiralled stone staircase leading to a second floor. The tight and precise spiral fit just inside the parameters of the vertical cylindrical library, with the spiral turning back on itself round to the right leaving a space underneath it that the girl had to question whether or not she would be required to duck under. The spiral then continued back around to the left above its entry on the ground floor. Covering perhaps sixty percent of the walls on the bottom floor of the library were raw wood bookshelves, in some cases from floor to ceiling. It was however to the girl's surprise that the shelves were almost entirely bare. Though this was in keeping with the rest of the house it was in contradiction to the library that featured in the girl's visions, and she had a strong feeling that the room held some sort of strong importance, but if the importance didn't lie in the books, then what else could it be? She pictured Greed's room in her mind but could not recall there being any books in there at all, adding to her puzzlement. To her right was a small desk area with two seemingly relatively newly lit candles upon it, situated underneath more bookshelves, again all but empty. The girl peered round under the spiral staircase to her left, spotting the library-keeper sitting on a pillowed rustic wooden bench positioned up against the wall. Without hesitation the girl stomped over to the library-keeper still fueled by her growing frustrations and impatience. She stood in front of her, towering over the relaxed-looking library-keeper sitting on the tassel-cushion covered bench.

"Where are all the books?" the girl queried with a sense of authority.

"Good morning, how are you feeling today?" the woman responded, one leg crossed over the other and hands politely on top of them, displaying a kind smile underneath her freckled nose and dainty wireframe glasses. The girl, realising her own rushed impoliteness recoiled slightly, taking a softer stance.

"I feel okay thank you," she responded, keeping a semi-stern face. "So where are all the books?" she asked again.

"What do you mean? All the books you need right now are here," the woman replied, without breaking her calmness in the slightest. 'That's enough', the girl thought to herself decidedly. As mild rage grew over the girl's delicate innocent features of her face, she turned at once and marched out of the library, almost stumbling down the jaunting stone step on her way out. 'I'm not doing this anymore, this is a stupid dream and it's time I woke up,' the girl continued her impassioned internal dialogue and continued her determined march through the front room and out through the front door. Unsure of what she was going to do next, she marched out onto the gravel path and onto the lush sole-tickling green grass beside it, towards the edge of the land. Was she going to jump?

Boiling in frustration the girl arrived at the edge in a cognitive instant, still not even aware of what she was aiming to do. She reached the edge, her toes curled over the grass lip that created an abrupt and illogical border, almost touching the mudrock infested dirt on the underside of it.

"Wait!" the girl heard a last-gasp cry from behind her. From the harmonically distressed high-pitch tone the girl sensed it must be Libi. Perhaps she was warning her of a ghastly mistake. She turned in order to find out, but it was too late, and as she turned the momentum of her bodyweight took her over the grassy border. As she fell, seemingly in fateful slow-motion, she could see all of the other house members, even the cat, gathered side by side outside the front door of the house, who could only watch on hopelessly as the girl fell and was sucked into the ambiguity of the clouds beneath.

IV. Rebirth

Laying on a patterned antique rug positioned in the centre of an ordinary, rectangular-shaped room was a girl, the same girl. Same girl, same rug, same room. Before the girl ventured to try and open her eyes she felt the tightly woven texture of the rug, which felt slightly more prickly than she remembered, and prayed that she was not back in the same place again. 'Surely not,' she thought to herself with a stomach-full of nervous anticipation. She apprehensively prised her eyelids apart at a gingerly pace, to reveal a blank white ceiling above her. There was not much to go off there, although she realised begrudgingly that she was in the same lying down position as the previous time. In a hopeful flash the girl thrust her upper body up off of the floor and leaned onto her elbows as support. As she looked in front of her and in her periphery it was immediately obvious to her where she was. The girl felt a concoction of emotions all at once, fear, confusion and anger to name a few. Sat across from her again with its back to the wall was the black and white cat, its hairs stood ever so slightly on end. The girl locked eyes with the cat, but their staring contest was cut short as the cat let out an intimidating hiss directed toward the girl and sprinted off into the kitchen. Perhaps it was reflecting the emotions of the girl right back at her. Her determination appears to have subsisted through her fall off of the island and subsequent resurrection, as she wasted no time in climbing to her feet in the search for answers. Proceeding to retrace her steps from before (whether consciously or not), the girl first headed purposefully to the kitchen, stopping to a halt in the doorway. Just like before, the chef stood slicing vegetables looking down at the chopping board, without acknowledging the girl's presence.

"Hello, can you please tell me what's going on here? Where am I? Who am I? How do I get out of here?" The girl demanded answers from the chef with a slightly raised voice.

"Ha Ha Ha Ha Ha," the chef chuckled in a belittling fashion. Again he did not look up from his knife and slightly dampened rustic wood chopping board. The knife seemed to gleem even more than before under the light, making it appear deathly sharp.

"Please answer me," the girl insisted, with despair. The chef paused abruptly mid-slice, lifting the knife off of the board and looking up at the girl.

"Don't worry, you're safe here with us," the chef declared. He smiled, as he did before, only this time it made the girl feel different. It was a smile tinged with a sinister feel, an ominous deceitfulness about it. The girl found this uncomfortable, and to her the chef looked exactly the same as before, yet somehow indistinguishably different at the same time. She concluded that her downward-spiralling emotions were probably causing her to just read things differently. This was a fair assumption to make, and the chef was likely being just as friendly as before, although this didn't stop the girl from feeling on-edge. With synchronised glints in his smile, eyes and the knife, the girl accepted his lack of information with disdain and decided to head to look outside, hoping that something may at least be different out there. With continued purposefulness the girl paced towards the front door, and twisted open the cold octagonal black metal doorknob. Stepping outside, the sharpness of the dull gravel path beneath her feet made her wince, and she picked up her right foot to see a singular dribble of blood run down the sole of her foot from the ball to the heel from a tiny pin-prick cut made from one of the jagged stone pieces. Again unsure if her perceptions were being influenced by her own mood, the air felt just a tiny bit colder and less inviting, the sky slightly darker, redder even, perhaps. To some the difference would not have even been distinguishable, but the atmosphere had an intangibly uncomfortable quality to it that the girl had not noticed before. Nevertheless, the girl took very little notice as she was much more intent on the visible aspects of her surroundings on the island, which, at first glance, looked identical. With everything looking the same as before, barring some minor atmospheric changes that the girl disregarded as insignificant extraneous detail, the girl headed back inside after taking a small loop a few strides in circumference around the gravel path to look around, without barely breaking stride. Continuing to retrace her initial steps from previously, the girl reentered the house and headed down the corridor on the right. The soft blue carpet she had remembered as being so soft and luxurious from before did not feel quite the same. It was still soft and comforting, and had it not been for its distinctly remarkable texture previously it may not have been a noticeable difference. On noticing this difference in sensation beneath her feet, the girl started to feel more on-edge, like something had changed, something wasn't quite right. Her stomach beginning to fill up like a tank with a saturating queasiness, the girl attempting to brush her apprehensions to the side, believing that these details still did not matter and were still merely extraneous detail to this hellhole from which she would soon escape.

The girl entered the lounge, with the intention of interrogating the bedraggled man on the sofa. The lounge too looked the same as she remembered, bare walls, bare shelves, an unlit smooth stone fireplace and surrounding brick chimney breast, and a high-backed antique sofa under the window, whereupon it lay the man, still. As before, the clock hanging above the fireplace was still motionless and its skinny hands fixed on 'XII'. The room was being lit by the backdrop of the midday sky through the window, which at certain angles appeared more hazy and yellowy-red than before. With his physical appearance identical to before (humorously 'smart casual' and scruffy), it appeared as though the man, as expected, had not moved an inch, why would he have?

"I need some answers," said the girl assertively, standing a few paces away from the sofa and the man, facing directly at him.

"Mmm," the man grunted lazily with his mouth kept shut, as if to say 'Go away, I'm resting!'.

"No, I've had enough, what is this place?" the girl asked with a growing temper. As her anger grew her attention focused on the man entirely, her supposedly irrelevant surroundings began to fade, and her whole body became warmer. The slight wrinkles on her head grew deeper as she frowned with displeasure and her fists tightened. At last the man showed signs of movement, with a seemingly burdensome effort he opened his eyes and looked straight at the girl. His glaring eyes felt as though they pierced straight through the girl for a moment. She sensed evil in his mottled and slightly misshapen grey irises, but she also sensed truth, a dormant ability or knowledge, giving her hope. His long greying hair dangled over his face.

"You will find the truth, and we will have fun showing it to you, ha ha," the man spoke with a hoarse throat and slight wheeze, looking somewhat excited and enthused by the girl's presence. "It is up to you to find out what is right and what is wrong, and if you don't, well, then I guess in answer to your question: this is your eternity, ha ha ha," the man continued on in a rambling fashion, experiencing clear enjoyment coming from projecting his crazed riddles. The man then re-crossed his arms and laid his head back down on the sofa, closing his eyes with an appearance of contentment. Standing still, perplexed and now equally fearful and annoyed, the girl tried desperately to think of what to say back.

"Who are you?" she blurted back, not content with this question but seemingly all she could muster at this moment. She waited for a few seconds but the man did not so much as flinch in any efforts to give a response. The girl scanned his body with her eyes up and down, noticing a frayed hole in his right leather shoe, with his big toe poking out, covered in a sock, thankfully. For some reason it was this that took the girl's frustrations over the edge, and she stormed out of the room with heavy footsteps, having had enough of the man's riddles and rudeness. Knowing that Libi had previously been the most helpful of the house members, she turned right out of the lounge door and hastily down the corridor toward Libi's room. As soon as she arrived at her door she felt her brash determination dissolve into an insecure timidness, which also allowed for the mild stinging sensation from the small cut on the ball of her foot to be brought to the girl's attention. She rubbed her foot on the carpeted floor until she felt the heat of friction on her sole, hoping that this would stop the bleeding. As she did so, she noticed that she had left a trail of tiny dots of blood all the wall up to Libi's door from the corridor. The girl took a few moments to compose herself, trying to convince herself that she would not let the strange people of this unexplainable floating house affect her anymore. With that thought, she raised a brave fist to Libi's door and with a rush of courage slapped her knuckles upon the painted wood, creating a mildly loud dull knocking noise. Before she had even completed three short knocks of the door, it flung open, to reveal Libi stood eagerly in anticipation. She was dressed the same as before, but perhaps every-so-slightly perceivably more flauntingly. Perhaps her ruffled red skirt was a centimeter or two higher, or perhaps her nails were painted a slightly deeper colour of red than before, matching the blood seeping from the girl's right foot. Either way, once again the girl was somewhat taken back by Libi's prominent beauty and momentarily lost for words. Needless to say, the feeling was mutual, Libi was clearly enamoured by the girl, to an extent that was now not being so easily hidden, and in fact was starting to look like an obsession.

"Hey, I've been waiting for you," said Libi with a devilish yet harmless smile. She outstretched her left arm and hand in a friendly offering to the girl. Without thought, and still lost for words, the girl reciprocated Libi's gesture and stuck out her right hand carefully into Libi's. For a moment it looked as though it was a mirrored image, the girl looking at her own reflection and taking her own hand in support, perhaps because this is what she needed the most right now. Then, in an instant and with strong muscular force, Libi pulled the girl toward her into a comforting embrace, pulling the whole of the girl's torso, legs and feet into her bedroom. The girl felt a little disconcerted, but ultimately gave in to the warm sanctuary of a loving hug – something that she had definitely needed. For a few moments it felt like bliss, like she was back in the arms of a loved one, finally safe again. After a few seconds Libi reasserted her surprisingly deceiving muscular strength and, still within the warming embrace, began to push the girl back, closing her bedroom door behind her and pushing her up against it, somewhat forcefully. Libi's curtains were fully closed, blocking out all natural light. The red walls created a red glow consuming the room as the light from her bedside lamp reflected off of it menacingly. Libi pulled her head back, looked at the girl, who now looked faintly fearful and unsure, looking her right in the eye. Libi quickly leaned in and attempted to kiss the girl. Their lips had barely touched before the girl brought an immediate end to the bizarre moment of passion by pulling her head away and gasped with an outburst of confusion;

"What are you doing?!"

"I'm sorry," responded Libi, maintaining the devilish smile upon her deep pink lips. "I thought it was what you wanted," she added, her smile turning more sinister by the second. The girl used both of her forearms to push Libi away from her, who attempted to keep the girl in her arms for just a couple of seconds longer, before giving in to the girl's desire for personal space. The girl looked at Libi, who appeared to be in a semi-crazed state of lust for her, but was thankfully calming down, before looking around Libi's room and noticing the same artwork dotted across the walls as before. Some pieces the girl recognised as beautifully painted landscapes, as well as the mildly erotic pieces she had also spotted before. This time however, she noticed some pieces of art with a much darker tone, some even fear-inducing. Creepy, deranged scribbles and paintings, mainly of various red and black colouring, some more detailed than others, and some seemingly more erratically sketched than others, that she did not see before. Did she really miss these last time? Now she had noticed them, they seemed too bold and terrifying to miss, so she thought that perhaps Libi had done them in the meantime, or moved their positioning, at least. Looking back and Libi, who now displayed a more neutral look upon her face, the girl, frightened and needing to recoup, leant her left hand on the doorknob of the door she was still stood up against and tried to twist it, indiscreetly, hoping somehow Libi wouldn't notice and that she could make a dash for it. She attempted to twist it left, and then right, but it wouldn't turn even slightly. 'Shit, it must be stuck,' she thought to herself, with panic ensuing. 'Or has Libi trapped me in here on purpose?' she questioned to herself, her paranoia growing in equal measure with the disturbing smile on Libi's face, which was now returning in great force. A reminiscent smell of Libi's strong perfume and a lingering scent of incense filled the girl's nostrils and lungs, almost making her begin to choke. Libi's smile was turning demented, her torso and head creating a sinister black shadow behind and above her. Short of breath, the girl twisted the doorknob more frantically and even turned to use both hands as she attempted to escape.

V. Apotropaic

Libi casually saunters over to the frantically distressed girl at the door, her footsteps reverberating around the hellish room. With one easy smooth motion Libi reaches out, grasps the doorknob and twists clockwise once and opens the door inwards. Moving back jumpily to get out of the way, the girl watches Libi open the door with ease and then turn to face her.

"You must have not been pulling hard enough," Libi said. "Got yourself in a bit of a mess there," she added. The girl realised immediately, her eyes locked with Libi's beautiful green pearlescent eyes, that she must have mistaken Libi's continuingly friendly smile with a more sinister grin. After a few moments the girl was able to calm her nerves enough to reciprocate, and the two beamed smiles back and forth, the girl's smile developing mostly out of relief than anything else, whereas Libi seemed to have been enjoying every moment. "Don't worry, you're safe here with us," Libi attempted to reassure the girl, but as she uttered the exact same words as the chef had to her not so long ago she experienced a strange sensation, as if all of the house members spoke the words to her at the same time. It brought an image to her mind of all of them standing side by side staring inward at her, projecting the message to the girl with a jarring echo, and although it was intended to be reassuring and perhaps should have been, it instead made the girl feel relatively uneasy. Not only did she hear them saying it, she felt it too. This was enough to make the girl abruptly exit Libi's room, the now fully open door being a fine invitation. Once she had exited the room, she turned to look at Libi, unsure of what to say and still quite shaken.

"Let me know if you need anything," Libi thankfully interrupted the girl's mental search for appropriate words.

"Thanks," the girl responded timidly and unsure, but happy to be out of Libi's room. Libi closed her door with noticeable force, enough to make the mild slam of its closure uncomfortable to the girl. 'Is she mad?' the girl thought to herself, but with little interest in finding an answer to her question she turned to look at the rest of the room behind her. It was to her surprise that she observed that the archway to the secondary corridor that led to Greed's room and the bathroom was no longer there. The wall which it was previously cut out was now a solid flat white wall with the continuing orange peel texture across it. Instead the girl noticed that there was an archway entrance to what appeared to be a separate corridor in the back right corner of the room, leading down the side of what was her bedroom. In her vehement haste earlier she had not noticed these subtle and intriguing alterations. With a moderate cautiousness in her step the girl strode over to the wall in front of her to where the archway used to be, and smoothed her hand all over the textured wall. Right to left and back again at chest height, and then even crouching and repeating the same motion at a lower level, the girl inspected the wall with great intrigue, gently pushing it as she did so to check its sturdiness and legitimacy. It felt just like a normal wall, as it looked. Puzzled, but in admittance that it was merely one more nonsensical aspect of the place she had unexplainably woken up in now multiple times, the girl wasted little time in questioning the oddity before making a beeline for the newly formed archway and corridor to her left. Upon entry to the dimly lit and suffocatingly narrow corridor the girl saw a door at the end of it directly ahead of her. Unsurprisingly it looked as innocuous as all of the other doors. About half way down the corridor on the right was yet another archway. Seemingly without acknowledgement of the increasingly ridiculous nature of the layout of this house, the girl continued down the corridor, sweeping her feet across the continuing blue carpet, which the more she walked on began to feel rather uncomfortably coarse. The archway to her right appeared to lead to another large square room which too was dimly lit, and if it weren't for its barren nature would have likely been decorated by a number of haunting silhouettes and shadows. Unenthused by the room's unremarkable appearance, the girl chose to instead go for the door at the end of the corridor. The second half of the corridor seemed darker, ominously so. With each step the floor seemed to get colder, the air thinner and the girl's anxiety more pronounced. Managing to keep her emotions somewhat contained, the girl approached the door and after some understandable hesitation proceeded to knock three times. Her expectations of a response were especially low, approaching non-existent, and she quickly repositioned her body in an effort to prepare to open the door. To the girl's shock the doorknob turned and the door shunted open in a flash.

"What do you want?" a voice emanated from a dark figure who stood behind a small head-width opening in the door. Even in combination, the lighting from the corridor and the light from the room in front were too dim to illuminate the figure's face or any bodily features. From the raspiness and insecurity within his voice the girl assumed it was Greed. Was he so embarrassed from what the girl had seen of his room earlier that he was now hiding from her? And to address the bigger question, why and *how* had his room moved?

"Greed...?" the girl whispered sympathetically.

"Yeah it's me," he responded rather impatiently.

"Why has your room moved? And why won't you show your face?" the girl asked with both confusion and compassion. Begrudgingly Greed took this prompt and opened the door further, revealing his face enough from the shadows to be recognised. Behind him the girl noticed a similar but perhaps more extensive and lucrative pile of items in his room, stacked up high against the walls, on his bed and other furniture, towering over his short figure from the girl's perspective, and almost making it all the way to where Greed was now hunched over at the door.

"Stop looking. It's mine." Greed announced to the girl feistily, eager to protect the wildly varied possessions in his dimly-lit dungeon of a room.

"O-okay, sorry," the girl uttered back gingerly. She had little interest in the items in the room and no intent on stealing any of them, and was much more interested in finding out why the room had moved. 'Did I just remember the layout wrong?' she questioned herself, beginning to doubt her own sanity. 'It's possible, given what has happened to me here,' she concluded, rather rashly.

"I like your ring," Greed spoke, suggestively, an apparent glint of hunger in his eyes, pointing a bony-knuckled outstretched finger toward her left hand. 'Ring?' the girl thought and reacted somewhat bemused. The girl looked down at her left hand and there upon the ring finger of her left hand was a lavish silver ring, embellished with a round cut black diamond at its centre. 'What…? How?' the girl froze and pondered to herself. She had never seen this ring before, and she was certain that she wasn't wearing it earlier. Possessing and imposing and mystifying beauty, the girl couldn't help but experience simultaneous awe and complete bewilderment at the polished item of bijouterie. 'Could this be a clue?' she wondered, 'could this help me get out of here?', thoughts rushed to her mind. She flexed her fingers as if to test its authenticity and she felt the solid silver pinch the skin on her finger slightly. It was real. But how had it got there? The girl found herself overwhelmed by a ball pit of unexplained mysteries around her. The room began to spin and the already narrow walls of the corridor started to close in like a scene in a horror movie. She became dizzy, nauseous and panicked. Experiencing momentary black outs and with the room's orbit of her accelerating, the girl slumped to the floor. Her ears were ringing, her whole body had gotten hot, and she felt as though she may vomit.

Eventually from her disabling state on the floor she was able to gradually recover, the orbit of the room slowed, the blackouts stopped, and the nausea somewhat subsided, although this remained with her to a certain degree for quite some time. When her senses had returned close enough to normal for her to drag herself to her feet using the textured walls of the corridor, she noticed that Greed's door was closed, and he was gone. He had left her in this state, more interested in protecting his plentiful possessions than helping the girl. This girl found this odd, as she had felt a pleasant connection toward Greed the previous day, and he, like the others, had presented himself as rather friendly and welcoming. After clambering to her feet the girl took a short while to reassess her situation. She considered the completely absurd nature of what was currently her reality. An unexplained floating house in the sky with five house members that seemed to have awfully fluctuating moods and with severe reluctance to provide her with any useful information. Certain rooms in the house appeared to potentially be moving positions, with the fireplace and the library being assumably important features. 'Where on earth am I, seriously?' the girl thought to herself in some distress. 'Who am I?', 'How can I escape?'. The girl really began to question her own sanity, and how this situation was even possible, a dream still the most plausible explanation to her. The same questions rattled around the girl's mind for some time, her complete perplexedness running in parallel to her low-lying nausea. The girl concluded that the most likely place for her to find a physical way off of this floating island would surely be outside, and so with this thought she mustered up the confidence and energy in her weakening condition and headed back down the gloomy corridor, using the wall in some places to support her bodyweight as she experiences waves of extreme fatigue in her legs. Then she crept silently past Libi's room, not wanting to deal with her overbearing and previously scary personality at this moment, and as she approached the entrance to the other corridor she noticed that the small blotches of blood on the carpet floor from the tiny cut on her foot had spread slightly and enlarged, perhaps tripling in diameter. Very slowly and quietly approaching these blotches, the girl attempted to pay close attention to their detail, but other than their expanded size, nothing seemed extraordinary about them. Remembering her mission, the girl disregarded the blotches of blood as another small oddity of the house, and continued down the corridor, trodding directly over the blood stains, proving her disinterest. By the time the girl had reached the end of the second corridor she was somewhat desperate for fresh air, after feeling rather claustrophobic inside the dingy and humid tunnels. It was to her relief that the front door was only a few steps away from the archway leading out of the corridor. The front door had been left marginally ajar and she could now feel, smell and taste the fresh air. Noticing from the crack in the door and the backdrop of the sky that it was now most likely mid-to-late afternoon, the girl thought to herself that the day seemed to be moving on rather fast, only further inspiring her efforts to escape as soon as she could. On route to the front door however the girl was stopped in her tracks as she heard a repetition of shrill smashing sounds coming from the kitchen. Every shattering smash was followed by a few seconds of silence and then a strange, indistinguishable dragging sound, like scraping a nail across bare wood, before the next almighty *smash!* Unable to resist her intrigue, the girl changed course and crept over to the kitchen door, pressing her face close up to the tiny opening in it. She deepened and slowed her breathing in order to remain as undetectable as possible. What she observed was yet another absurd and frightful sight. Hunched over the kitchen counter at which all the girl had seen him do was prepare vegetables, was the chef, with a variety of plates and dishes of food, immaculately and intricately prepared and displayed out in front of him on the wooden counter-top. One-by-one and with an evil grin of greed on his face the chef was dragging the china plates and glass dishes closer to his face, which was no more than a few inches off of the surface in his hunched stance, and proceeded to shove the food straight into his mouth using both hands, crazily chewing it and then swallowing rapidly, before shunting the plate off of the counter-top, which would then smash with some impact as it hit the floor. He appeared to be in an possessed animalistic state, unconscious of his surroundings, like a feral wolf in the middle of an indulgent feast under the backdrop of the afternoon sun barely lighting the cottage-style kitchen. Becoming uncomfortable with her rigid position, the girl attempted to adjust, taking another small step with her left foot, landing it on top of the polished plank of wood on the floor separating the kitchen and the front room. As she did so, she stepped down onto a sharp shard of something, presumably a piece of one of the plates that had been flung across the square-tiled floor of the room all the way to the door. It was extremely sharp and felt as though it had penetrated deep into the girl's foot, causing a shocking shooting pain which the girl could not fully contain. She winced expressively and as she did so knocked her right arm and leg into the kitchen door, making a banging noise while also pushing it open just a bit more. At once she noticed that the noise coming from the kitchen turned to silence, and she froze on the spot, holding her left foot in pain with both hands, and not letting herself make another noise. Her heart rate ran wild, and the girl had to fight everything in her body to maintain a steady and quiet breath. Even after waiting an uneasying amount of time in silence, the noise from the kitchen did not resume, and silence continued to consume the daunting house. Making the bold decision to turn and head for the front door, the girl hopped and hobbled away from the kitchen door. As she approached the front door she felt as if someone was chasing her menacingly, and envisaged an image of the chef scampering after her wielding his large shiny chef's knife, bearing an evil food-smothered grin, but her overwhelming fear meant that she resisted the urge to turn and check on the validity of her sixth sense. After flinging open the front door in desperation and jumping outside, the girl slammed the door behind her with such intent that it created a vacuum, sucking the girl's clothes back towards the door behind her. Off balance, the girl fell back against the front door and once again slumped to a crouched position on the gravel floor, resting her back against the upright wooden door. Although the girl needed some time to recoup, she was not afforded it as the gravel beneath quickly became far too pointed and sharp for her to continue sitting on. She quickly checked the sole of her left foot to search for the sharp object that she had just stepped on, but all she could see was blooded trickling from the stinging wound. Re-energising herself by convincing herself that she was about to find a way off of the island, the girl staggered to her feet and off of the uncomfortable gravel path as soon as possible. Once stood on the safe (for now) haven of the grass beside the path, the girl noted the simultaneous beauty and errieness of the hazy red-yellow tinged late-afternoon sky, noticing how it sat above and around her like poisonous gas. Mustering up more energy and enthusiasm, the girl paced swiftly around the island, looking for clues or items of notability in her attempt to escape. First heading to the farm area the girl noticed the bountiful nature of the crops that grew inside the wooden-fenced l-shaped area featuring an idyllic array of produce and seemingly perfect irrigation system, with its only entrance being on the left side opposite the farmer-style hut. The girl made her way around the left-hand side of the farm area, between the gate opening and the farmer-hut, around toward the section of fruit trees at the back of the island. Without getting particularly close to the dangerous edge, the girl scoured the area around and under the trees, at some points even crawling on her hands and knees in her efforts to find anything of interest. Nothing was to be found. In some moments being amongst the plants, grass and trees almost made the girl forget of her own whereabouts, and she was able to feel a certain sense of peace, with her fingers intertwined with the longish strands of green grass on the floor. After a considerable time of searching the girl stood up once more and looked up to the sky. Suddenly she realised just how dark it had become, and how strangely quickly this had happened. She found herself under the trees looking back at the house which emitted an uninviting red glow, surrounded by near complete-darkness. She also noticed just how bitterly chilled the air had become, creating quite an unsettling ambiance. It was at this point that she began to hear noises. Ranging from short and sharp high pitched squeaks to low and long rumbles, the noises began to plague the girl's paranoid mind, and she grew extremely anxious and fearful, feeling somewhat trapped in the abyssal darkness under the trees. She tried to remind herself that the noises were almost certainly her tired mind playing tricks on her, however this did not work and the girl's panic rose exponentially. Her mind was only eventually distracted when she noticed the same yellow-green bowl-sized glow coming from the farmer-style hut that she had seen the previous night. A moment later she perceived movement from inside the hut, a rough shuffling around, followed by a clatter of metal objects and then the gradual opening of the hut door, with an ominous creek that pierced the air straight to the girl's ears. The sound vibrated through the girl's body, succeeded by the scraping sound of metal along the concrete floor of the hut, and then two anticipatory boot stomps.

"Here here, where are you? I'll find you, I'm hungry," a deep and twisted voice came from the hut, the door now nearly fully open, followed by a cackle of laughter. To say this sent shivers down the girl's spine would be a huge understatement. Pausing to consider her best course of action, the girl held her position rigidly. Internally, adrenaline surged about the girl's body like never before.

"These aren't for you yet ha ha ha," the voice spoke again, becoming even more sinister with every word spoken, the sound of which warped in the girl's mind as she visualised it like a hypnotic swirl centering in on her anxiety. The shadow of the figure gestured towards the bowl-sized yellow-green glowing item, which was this time atop a bench of surface at about waist height. Then, the shadow shuffled left and heavy boots made more clomping noises as the figure took short shuffled strides towards and out of the thin wooden hut door, dragging a long metal instrument along the ground beside him, producing a constant eerily shrill ringing sound. 'Boots, long metal weapon, farmer's hut, it must be the gardener' thought the girl, and although he had always seemed relatively pleasant to her, this time she could tell something wasn't quite right. He was heading for her, and he seemed angry, vengeful even. At first the girl considered what she had done wrong to warrant any backlash from the gardener, although this line of internal questioning could not last long as the girl felt the impending importance of her next decision, which had to be quick. Firstly considering whether to simply turn around and jump off of the island for a second time, the girl decided instead just to run. Where? She didn't know, but she ran for her life, round the back of the farm area and back of the house, where her frenzied panic was met with almost pure darkness. A darkness in which she became immediately lost.

VI. Descendit ad Inferos

Disoriented, scared and hopeless, the girl dropped to her hands and knees and crawled forward into the darkness around the back of the house. It wasn't long before the fingertips of her right hand, feeling around on the floor in the dark in desperation, felt the sharp edges of the gravel path in front of her to her right. She knew that if she followed the path round the side of the house it would lead her back to the front door. However, not only was the gravel path too sharp to crawl on for a sustained period of time, she was also aware that doing this would only likely lead her back to the angry gardener, pitchfork in hand. Pausing for a moment to think, still on her hands and knees and vulnerable to the elements, the girl tried to picture the layout of the island and the house that she had explored so far. With this thought the girl was able to devise a secondary option. She had remembered that from Libi's bedroom window a large apple tree was visible, and that if she could find the apple tree she may be able to use it to find Libi's window, which she could knock on to alert Libi, who could then let her into her room. However the girl did not feel fully comfortable with this plan, as although Libi had in general been very welcoming and friendly towards her, her forceful nature earlier in the day resulted in quite a traumatic ordeal for the girl. She concluded however that a potential recurrence of an episode of Libi's overbearing emotions while inside the relative sanctity of her room was the lesser of two evils in her current scenario. As the girl attempted to work out how to locate the apple tree she remembered something even more important. It was just Libi's bedroom window that offered a view of the tree, but her own bedroom window did too! In fact her own bedroom window she now remembered provided an even fuller view of the tree than Libi's. Still unnervingly aware of her bleak and ominous surroundings, the girl crawled across the gravel path and onto the grass on the other side of it. Due to her lack of energy, the girl could only drag her hands and knees across the jagged splinters of gravel beneath her, tearing holes in her jeans and resulting in numerous slashes and cuts in her arms, hands and knees, like she had crawled across fifty metres of broken glass. The girl, now deep in determination toward the task ahead, barely battered an eyelid at the otherwise menacing injuries. As she dragged her heavy corpse-like body onto the grass, she could feel the slick glass wiping against the blood dribbling from her hands and knees, each blade individually licking the cuts and providing an additional eye-watering sting. After her whole body was upon the much nicer surface of the grass the girl collapsed onto her back, overwhelmed by confusion, panic and utter exhaustion. She laid on her back, mouth open, eyes glistening, staring at the sky above. With all four of her limbs outstretched randomly, sprawled out in a hopeless pose, the girl allowed herself a moment to recover. As her mouth began to dry and as she became paralysed in awe of the matrix of stars above her pin-pricked into the gloomy red-black night sky, she contemplated giving up. 'What would happen if I just laid here... forever?' the girl thought to herself. She was no longer scared or confused, only indifferent. As though she had finally stopped fighting her looming fate, it had stopped fighting her back, and allowed her this moment of peace.

A pessimistic dim glow of juxtaposed early morning air woke the girl gently. Surprisingly however the light was not coming from above, but instead from the open bedroom window to her right. The girl found herself back in her bed, in her bedroom. Confused, the girl attempted to hoist herself up to inspect the window, however the gusto with which she attempted to do so was soon thwarted by the stiffness of her knees. She winced as the multitude of platelet-sealed cuts cracked open as her knees hinged downward. Her hands similarly rigid from the mass of dried blood upon them had left handprint blood stains all over her ironed cotton sheets. Looking at the carpeted floor between the window and the bed however the girl could not discern any visible blood splatters or marks, which she considered strange as it would have been safe to assume that with the state of the cuts on her legs and hands that at least some blood would have made it onto the carpet during her journey from the window to the bed. Even more bemusing was the fact that the girl could clearly see a considerable amount of blood splattered and smeared around the window frame and window ledge, and even on the window itself, just nothing on the floor. While sat on the edge of her bed facing the window, her cut knees and legs dangling off the edge of the bed and her toes barely touching the carpet, the girl looked to her left to see that instead there was a trail of blood leading to the bedroom door, which itself had a bloodied handle. The girl sat, perplexed. It was as if two possible scenarios that had led to her waking up back in her bed unaware of exactly how she got there had... both happened? At first she felt sure that she must have climbed back through her bedroom window herself – hence the bloodstains all over it. However it was also possible, she admitted, that someone could have found her outside passed out on the grass, the gardener for example, and helped her back to her room – hence the bloodstains near the door. Upon imagining both scenarios independently, the girl found the second one considerably more spine-chilling. The girl managed to quickly put her mind at ease as she decided that the matter was rather irrelevant. All that currently mattered was that she was safe, and now had the chance to devise yet another plan.

While considering what to do next, the girl also noted that she did not know what time of day it was. She had no way of knowing how long she was asleep for. It was light, but with no sun in the sky to reference, it could be any time really between early morning or mid afternoon. This realisation further hurried the girl's decision making, as she assumed that whatever her plan was, it would be easier to carry out while it was still light. One fact could not escape the girl's mind, and that was that she had still not given the library a thorough look-over. She remembered the innate significance that she felt, for some reason, that the room held, and how it had appeared in her profound visions. However, the girl had been rather distracted by other matters since, understandable in her absurd situation. The utter delirium of her situation once again re-entered her thoughts, and a combination of confusion and frustration brought her to muffled tears. For a few moments the girl simply sobbed, feeling lost and hopeless. Adding to the severity of her distress was the further fact that the girl still did not know who she was, and where she was trying to get back to. All she had was a deep feeling that there was something else, somewhere else, that she belonged. Like Alice in Wonderland she was trapped down a rabbithole of the strange and unknown. Managing to recompose herself the girl knew that the library was currently her best option for finding a solution to her madness, and so with a collection of deep breaths and thoughts of encouragement over the space of half an hour or so of deep contemplation and inner-will grathering, the girl hopped to her scratched feet, disregarded her bloodied legs and arms, and walked toward her bedroom door. Knowing that admitting defeat was not an option, and that wallowing in her situation was certain not to help matters, the girl compiled every ounce of determination and bravery inside herself and bounded it into a thrust of faith, manifesting a confident thrust off of the bed and towards the bedroom door. The cuts in her knees were too painful to ignore, with every stride cold air filled the freshly split cuts like oil being added to a flame, and shot pain up the girl's legs, making her wince as she walked. After swinging open her bedroom door, the first thing that was projected upon the girl's attention was the carpet in the hallway room. The bloodied circles created from the minor drops of blood from the girl's foot had continued to transform in size, now appearing as two or three huge circular blood stains, taking up that entire corner of the carpet in the room. Having expanded potentially hundreds of times the size of the original dots of blood, the stains appeared like huge crop circles in the soft blue field of carpet, covering the carpet from the far entrance to the room ahead, up to Libi's door, and stretching out a third of the way into the centre of the room. Aghast, the girl took a moment to catch her breath, hanging onto her door frame, as if petrified to step out onto the carpet. As she stared at the devilish red circles, they began to pulsate, as if they were living, growing and shrinking with every rapid beat of the girl's heart. Simultaneously she felt her eyes pulsing, as if the blood vessels were copying the pulsating rhythm of the bloody satanic pools. It crossed the girl's mind to quickly run and jump over them without further thought, but instead, perhaps mesmerised in some way, she stepped out onto the carpet and took small but consistent steps towards them. Remarkably, and somewhat horrifyingly, she did not seem deterred by the vile squelching sounds from beneath her feet as she, after a few clean-carpeted steps, stood directly upon the blood stains. From each step emanated a sound similar to the stabbing sound effect used in the Scream franchise, yet the girl's pace did not slow, nor hasten. Transfixed on the blood-soaked floor beneath her feet, the girl looked down and all around her at the blood. She then noticed its temperature, which can only be described as warm, yet somehow still chilling to her feet, indescribable. It was at this moment that the girl was snapped out of her trance, as she began to hear gentle knocking coming from Libi's room. It sounded as though Libi was gently tapping on either her door or the wall, or both. As she walked a few extra steps, it seemed as though the sound followed the girl, deliberately so. Finding this intensely creepy, the girl held her breath and leaned closer to the wall. As the girl listened intently for the sound to continue, it in fact stopped, and Libi's door silently opened. Attempting to search for the sound, the girl took a couple of gentle steps back towards Libi's door, still fully immersed in the wall and unaware of the door's opening. As she did so, an arm crept out of Libi's room on the floor, around the door and through the small opening in the doorway. With the same deep red painted nails as Libi, yet a somewhat gloomier and more lifeless appearance, the arm, using its fingers like tiny legs, crept silently closer to the girl's right leg as she maintained her leaned stance toward the wall, also maintaining her lack of awareness of the situation. Inching closer to Libi's leg the fingertips of the outstretched arm dipped themselves into the pools of blood situated just outside Libi's bedroom. The arm then slithered back into the room through the doorway, again silently, and was followed by a heinous cackle from something within. Startled by the insidious chuckle the girl abruptly turned her neck to look to her right and Libi's door. In the same frightened breath Libi's bedroom door slammed closed, and this was again followed by a similarly heinous chuckle from within. The girl's attention was then, without notice, spun towards a voice in the opposite back corner of the room.

"I like your ring… Can I have it?". Greed stood in the dimly lit back corner of the room next to the entrance to the corridor leading onto his room. He spoke with a sinister intent, and it appeared as though all of his prior friendliness had been overtaken by his lust for the girl's jewellery upon her left ring finger. The girl looked down at the jewel, her reflection glistened back at her on the deep black gem. It felt like she was looking into her soul, but at the same time looking at a complete stranger, and she empathised with the fright and confusion she saw within herself. Without barely another moment passing Greed abruptly began tok stomp across the room, heading directly toward the girl, with evil in his eyes. The girl looked up at him marching towards her, and noticed her helpless reflection again, this time in Greed's eyes, that had turned into deep black marbles, almost two exact replicas of the black diamond jewel upon her finger. Instinctually the girl turned and ran, the heavy clomps of Greed's steps echoing behind her and reverberating throughout the house. She ran too quickly and frantically past the doorway to the lounge for any of its contents to appear as anything but a blur. Upon reaching the end of the corridor and the front room it led onto, she was once again stunned. The front room was no longer the front room. It was the… bathroom? Yet, even more bemusingly it had three doors flung wide open – one to the left, one straight ahead, and one to the right. The doors were the doors from the front room. In front of her was the heavy-looking rustic metal door with mediaeval stone doorframe, to her left was the front door leading out onto the floating island and subsequent abyss, and to her right the kitchen door, also wide open, but with no one in sight through it. The rest of the room was most definitely the bathroom, the same tiles, bath, mirror and sink. It was incredibly disorientating, and the girl began to feel dizzy and overwhelmed. The sheer force of the dizziness and confusion obliged her to close her eyes, and when she reopened them, she was back at the doorway to the front room – the *actual* front room. Her momentary feeling of relief was quickly muted by the resumption of the oncoming and terrifying unpleasant and daunting sound of Greed's marching footsteps. Blindly (although perhaps subconsciously remembering her plan) the girl darted jumpily toward the library door across the room from her. Frightfully skipping and hopping as if a dog were chasing her tail, she made it across the room, through the doorway and onto the painfully cold stone floor of the library, hurriedly using all of her strength to close the door behind her. To her luck (which she felt at this point she was due) the inside of the door has a long thick rectangular wooden beam horizontally across it that could act as a rudimentary barrier to prevent the door being opened from the other side. The girl wedged the beam between the door and the desk situated in the alcove to the right of the door, not knowing how much force it could withstand, but sincerely hoping for the best. Sweating from head to toe, the girl held still and quiet in anticipation of Greed's approach. He must have only been a few strides behind her as almost instantly he began banging at the door. He let out simultaneously grunts and moans, like that of a frustrated toddler who hadn't got his own way. His voice seemed to deepen with every moan and grunt, and so too did the banging noise. As the whole library began to vibrate, the girl prayed for it to end.

It did not take very long for Greed to give up. Within a minute the banging stopped and so too did the grunting and moaning. What ensued however was far more chilling. Greed began to sob. One moment it sounded almost as if a baby, fresh from the womb, was crying, almost screaming, on the other side of the door, and the next moment it sounded like exactly what it was, the deep haunting desperate cry of a fully-grown man. Every hair on the girl's body stood on its end like tiny pine needles, and she remained standing on the other side of the door, her toes almost frozen solid, completely unsure of what to do. But then, mid ear-piercing whine, abrupt silence fell upon her. Illogical. Total illogical silence.

VII. Gorgo

In the unremitting silence the girl was able to regain some composure. Wiping her clammy hands on her tattered denim jeans and for the first time acknowledging her painfully cold toes and soles, she turned, completing a steady one-hundred-and-eighty degree spin to assess the room. Rather uninteresting yet somewhat comforting it was that the library appeared exactly the same as before. It had a pleasant ambient glow about it, one that contrasted the aggressively cold nature of the floor and walls, and resultantly just about the entire room. The numerous cuts deep within the girl's knees, legs, arms and hands stung even more than before as her anxious sweat pooled in the gory crevices, accumulating to a pain more intense than the girl had ever experienced, or so she assumed. Actually, something had changed in the library, there were somehow more books. Not loads, just a few, placed neatly and sporadically around the various bookshelves that the girl could see in the lower portion of the room. With another sudden throbbing reminder of the temperature of her feet, the girl hopped daintily onto the thin antique rug that covered most of the library floor. She studied the rug's details for a moment, noticing how it was made up of delicate looking tapestries depicting almost biblical scenes, or at least a knock-off version of the sort. After further inspection it was clear they were not pleasant scenes whatsoever and in fact far more hellish and daunting than the rug's soft-enough texture would have suggested, and the girl's still fraught soul would have hoped for. Immediately intrigued by the additional books upon the shelves the girl approached the back wall of the library to further inspect. The first to grab her attention was a red leather book, dead centre in the middle of the bookshelf at eye-height, and as the girl leaned in and squinted she made out its title: 'Gospel Hymn Book'. 'Right, not much use,' she thought, feeling as if it could even be an attempt to mock her. Flicking her vision leftward she could see what she knew was a Bible at the far left end of the same shelf, without the need to get any closer, in pristine condition yet still somehow looking old and used. 'So I should pray to get out of here, is that it?' she thought to herself, sarcastically. She scoffed and looked right, to the other far end of the same shelf, at which she saw two books, coupled side by side, seemingly fatefully. 'Buddhism for beginners' stood next to 'Meditation for beginners', upright and once again in pristine condition. 'Hmm, more useful, perhaps, but not sure how,' the girl again whispered internally with a dying hope. Then, she heard a frightening hiss from above. She took a reactive step back away from the bookshelf and looked up. There it was again, the cat. Sat upon the top shelf, one above the one with the books on, looking down at the girl with evil green eyes and an asymmetric gnarly scornful grin. Behind it, a small crucifix made of what looked like simple wood, painted white, the paintbrush stroke marks visible. Either side of the cat, more books, the whole arrangement looking like some sort of Satanic shrine. 'How did I not notice the cat earlier?' the girl questioned to herself, once again bemused. The books on either side of the cat were as follows: 'Heaven and

Hell by Emanuel Swedenborg' and 'Inferno by Dante'. Unfortunately these did not mean much to the girl at this time, it was as if her memory had been wiped. She understood the concepts of heaven and hell and religion, but beyond that she could draw little meaning from the books just from their titles and well-kept covers. Cautious of a potential attack by the angry-looking feline friend (or perhaps more foe as it appeared now), the girl stood braced for a fight. All body hair once again stood on end, straight as a splinter from follicle to tip, and her toes curled slightly. However, as quickly as it had seemingly magically appeared, within the blink of the girl's tired and wrinkled eyes, the car was gone. For a moment the girl felt somewhat silly, stood in the middle of the library in some sort of makeshift jiu-jitsu style pose looking as if she was ready to attack some old books upon shelves hanging from an old stone brick wall. She quickly resumed a normal pose, long and thin like a solitary sardine in a big stone brick tin. She appeared to be getting thinner by the hour, her body losing colour, too. It also ached, from head to toe, and if it weren't for the girl's continuing determination, this would surely be a sorry and incomplete end. She took another step closer to the books, resuming her previous position before she was rudely startled by the car, or some imagined version of the cat, at least. As part of the stride forward her nostrils were invaded by the familiar waft of vanilla scented lignin and leather, which immediately evoked an image in the girl's head. An image of someone. 'The librarian!', the girl exclaimed, again internally. It seemed as though physical speech was perhaps too energy-consuming for the girl to now muster. After her eureka moment, at once the room felt as though a clouded haze came over it, floating about the girl's head. 'Is it getting hotter in here?' the girl thought, while beginning to pant and thrust her blouse top back and forth on her chest in an effort to remain cool. The floor and walls remained paradoxically bone-cold. It was as if someone had turned up the thermostat, and it was accompanied by pressure, an increase thereof. The librarian was not sitting on the bench to the left of the room underneath the spiral staircase where she had sat previously, but the girl could now feel her presence. She was in the library, the girl felt eerily certain of it. Despite her conscious better judgement the girl moved towards the spiral staircase and ventures a solitary first step onto the ice cold two-foot wide stone slab that comprises the first step of the staircase. She pauses, expectant of movement or sound from above, but nothing. With a much required deep exhalation of breath the girl takes a second step, this time her right foot making the courageous journey a foot higher in altitude to the step above. During another anticipatory pause the deathly silence is acknowledged by the girl. Even her own footsteps could not be heard. Deciding that it could be wise to try and hurry the process of ascending the stairs slightly, the girl took the next few steps in quick succession, climbing enough stairs to enable her to peer around the corner of the spiralling grey stone slabs and up into the top floor of the library. The slabs were so washed and dull in their grey shade they appeared anaemic. With an aching back and neck the girl peered over the top step, but from her disadvantaged vantage point she was unable to discern much else than a similarly hazy glow of light as below and yet more bookshelves, covering the entirety of the left and back walls that she could see. Now on her hands and knees across a few middle steps in the staircase, the girl thought it a good idea to scamper up the remaining slabs, encourage firstly by the fact that she had not seen anything up there as of yet to perturb her, and secondly by the inner thought that if someone, or something, was waiting for her, she could obtain the upper-hand with an element of haste and surprise. Thirdly, the (literally) stone cold slabs were really beginning to cause serious discomfort for the girl's already bruised hands and feet. Mid-scamper she could feel the dust collecting in her fingertips and palms from the top few steps. She was hesitant to look around until she reached the top step, scared even to look to her left and right. Upon reaching the top floor she decided she had no choice but to look around, firstly to her right. This floor was much more open than the bottom, stretching away to her right, this time with wooden floorboards topped by a similar antique rug as the floor below. The rug guided the girl's vision toward the end of the room to her right, where upon another simple oak wood bench sat the librarian, one beige tight-covered leg over the other, stroking the aggressively poised cat upon her knee like a Bond villain. Looking calm and sure of herself the librarian stared at the girl as if she was looking into her soul, causing the girl to experience a winding of sorts in her belly as she stared back. The silent stare-off continued for such an extent of time that it became almost awkward.

"Uhh… Hi," the girl muttered, hesitantly as blood dripped from her knees – the sight of which the cat appeared to be licking its lips.

"It's about time you were here," replied the librarian, sternly and pompously as she continued to stroke the snarling cat. The girl looked around the room while attempting to keep one eye on the untrustworthy lady and cat. It was relatively boring, behind her being a back wall just a few paces away again mostly covered by a bookshelf up to head height. Directly above her the castle turret-like building was topped by a grandiose dome of stained glass. Beautifully the stained glass seemed to complete the night sky, its design featuring a moon, sun and a multitude of dazzling colours interspersed with various religious and mythical representations.

"Could you help me with the books?" the girl asked, politely. "Can they help me? and if so how? and which ones?" the questions poured out of the girls mouth like boiling water out of an overspilling kettle.

"Ha! Why would I help you?" the woman responded. "If I were you I would give up… accept your fate" she added, a sinister grin growing across her face as she spoke.

"My… fate? What do you mean?" the girl queried, terrified and confused.

"'Depart from me, you cursed, into the eternal fire prepared for the devil and his angels'" the woman spoke, straight faced, without emotion. Under her breath she continued to mumble what sounded like threatening Biblical verse in condemnation toward the girl. The girl screwed up her face in confusion, before deciding to ignore the crazed librarian. She turned to her left to inspect the books. As she did so the wood beneath her feet began to feel more splintered, uncomfortably so, a single step to her left toward the bookshelf felt like a step onto a bed of nails. With this too the temperature again began to rise, the wood beneath her beginning to feel as if it were soaked in warm water. On the shelf sat just one book. 'Limbo'. The white writing revealed its title unassumingly on its plain black spine. Before the girl had even had the thought to pick up the book, the librarian interjected.

"The books must not leave the library," she stated imposingly, like she had predicted the girl's next move. Flicking her vision momentarily to the librarian, who held her pose, and then back to the book, the girl followed an impulse in her head to grab the book and run. In a flash she was off, down the spiral staircase, almost launching herself to injury down the hard stone slabs. In her descent, a quick glance up and backward revealed to her an impossibly horrifying metamorphosis of the librarian. Her shoulder-length mousy brown hair had transformed seemingly instantaneously into hungry-looking serpents with piercing bright red eyes and long forked tongues. 'What the fuck is that?' the girl internalised her panic and maintained her bolt toward the door. The snakes most definitely were chasing after her as if attempting to enforce the eighth commandment 'Thou shalt not steal'. Without the girl noticing until now the library had continued to increase in temperature, now feeling as though the whole library was going up in flames, although it wasn't. When the girl reached the door she found that her previous fortune had now been turned against her as she struggled to remove the heavy wooden beam from across the door. This gave the girl a moment to consider what she had just seen, and as she scrambled in panic to move the heavy splintering beam from behind the door with the backdrop of approaching angry hisses in her ears, she concluded she must have actually gone mad. Not wanting to risk finding out if her sanity was in fact still intact and she was indeed being chased by a dozen shape shifting snakes, as soon as she managed to free the movement of the door from the wooden beam behind it, she yanked open the door and sprinted through its opening. She did so in such haste that she had forgotten the rather large step proceeding it into the front room, and as she launched herself off of it she came tumbling down onto her knees. Not only did this further exacerbate her panic and her fear of what could be coming increasingly close behind her, her unhealed knees were also ripped apart. Excruciating pain matches the abundant flow of bright red blood from her knees which was pumped out in rhythm with her heartbeat. Without time to even look at her wounds, the girl clambered to her feet and ran. 'Where can I go?' the girl thought to herself as she sprinted for the corridor opposite, clenching the book tightly in the left hand and pressing it against the outside of her leg for added security, or perhaps more as a representation of her achingly tense, anxious body. Sprinting with every bit of energy she had left, the girl took a sharp left up the corridor and reached the end of it in no time. While sprinting past the opening to the lounge she noticed the fire burning fiercely once again, feeling its radiating heat down her right side almost to the point of a burning pain, even in the tiny amount of time it took her to pass the doorway. Running toward and through the archway at the end the girl noticed something unexpected below her feet. Cold tiles. Cold small rectangular tiles. She looked down quickly. Blue small rectangular tiles. She looked back up. It was the bathroom. Once again she found herself in the bathroom, looking the same as before. Turning back, she looked down the corridor from which she had just entered to see a horrifying sight. On her trail was the chef, gardener, librarian, Greed, Liby, the cat, and even the man from the sofa in the lounge, all stood in the corridor at slightly different points so that they each had a view of the girl. At first the girl assumed they were coming towards her, each one with their own evil smile and stood or crouched in an hauntingly unnatural pose, coming to get her. Her reaction was to sprint towards the door and attempt to slam it shut and find a way of locking it to keep them out. However, as she arrived at the door she noticed that none of them were moving. In fact, they were all eerily still, just staring at her, creepy grins from cheek to cheek. After a second or two of baffled reciprocated stare, the girl slammed the door and locked it using the handily placed old metal key already inside the lock.

"What the fuck is going on?" the girl questioned, this time aloud, in a hushed frustrated voice. Almost in reaction to her bemused inquiry there was an immediate collective chuckle from the other side of the door. A twisted, evil raucous of laughter that sounded as though it was directly behind the door. 'Shit,' the girl really began to panic. If it wasn't for the lack of time to think and her last remaining supply of adrenaline coursing through her, the girl would have surely broken down into tears. She was petrified.

VIII. REST

Wanting, understandably, a further layer of security, not trusting the single wooden bathroom door and lock's ability to protect her for long, the girl turned around and looked for a solution. Immediately she was reminded of a potentially crucial piece of the puzzle – the secret boarded up room behind the bath. Firstly, she had to move the bath, this was no easy feat in itself. Around fifty kilograms of porcelain coated cast iron to haul, inch by inch, moving the bottom end out and allowing access to the boarded up door it was attempting to conceal. After squeezing herself into the gap she had created between the door and the bath, the girl looked around the bathroom for tools, before long notices a crowbar, conveniently placed next to her feet at the boarded up doorway. She was sure that it wasn't there originally, but she also did not care. While attempting to leverage open the diagonal planks concealing the mystery door, the girl began to try and comprehend the fact that she was even in the library. She was sure that the room she was running into at the end of the corridor was the square-shaped hallway room that led onto her and Libi's. Cutting her thinking short was the unwanted sound of banging on the bathroom door. Sporadic and without pattern the banging gradually intensified, hurrying the girl in her efforts to remove the wooden planks. Quite a mess was being created as she managed to crack open the first plank, shards of dried white paint crumbling off. The plank almost snapped in half rather than coming off nicely in one piece, suggesting it had been there some time. The second plank followed suit rather quickly, as if the girl had got the hang of using a crowbar. Digging her nails into the top of the now fully revealed door, the girl slowly pried it open, with some discomfort as her nails began to bend and snap under the force. They, like the rest of her body, had become much more brittle, so it seemed. Taking the crowbar with her as a seemingly futile offering of protection, the girl shoved herself through a small opening in the door before pulling it closed behind her, again with agonising effort. Inside the room it was pitch black. She could not see a single thing. The girl could not help but consider that this may have been the wrong decision coming here, yet she knew it also felt like her only choice. Moments later, banging on the door. 'What? They're in already?' the girl thought, worryingly. But after a few more seconds of banging, the girl realised that this time the banging was much more organised and in rhythm, and it sounded different. Each bang was centralised to one pin-head spot on the door, three of so at a time, and then over to another spot. The sound spread from each point like ripples on water. They were nailing the door back shut. She knew it. Pusing on the door firmly to see if it could be opened, the girl confirmed her fears. Panic ensued. 'If they are out there locking me in, then what if there is something far worse in here?' the girl thought to herself, sweat rushing down her body, her fingernails, knees, hands, legs and head all throbbing with pain. Managing to calm herself enough to attempt to assess the room, the girl did what most of us did as children when we suspected a monster underneath our bed, she stayed as still and as quiet as possible, hoping that the monster would leave her alone.

The banging stopped and was followed by a ceremonious laughter, again collective and perceivably sinister in nature. In the next moment, silence followed. Another bout of deathly silence, the type that the girl was not sure how much more of which she could take. Although acknowledging its uselessness in these light conditions, the girl gingerly felt about by her side for the book, unsure if she had remembered to bring it through the door with her. To her mild surprise there it was, down by her left side as it was before, although not as tightly pressed. The girl went back to remaining as still and quiet as possible, and began to ponder on some of the other books she had seen in the library, what they could possibly mean, and more pertinently of what use to her they could be.

After considering the general theme of the books she had seen on the library's barren dusty wooden shelves the girl came to a worrying initial hypothesis. She knew that the book seemed to be centred around religion, particularly Christianity, with references of the notions of heaven and hell also featuring. With her mind allowing her access to the recollection of the basic concepts of heaven and hell but little other details from memory, the girl began to consider the possibility that perhaps that is where she currently was, but which one? Accepting this as a possibility also meant that the girl had to accept the possibility that she may therefore be dead, which was understandably a scary and intimidating thought, and the girl struggled to contain her panic and anxiety at this idea. In her entirely dark and silent surroundings the girl felt as if had been buried alive, which, she considered, would make sense if her previous hypothesis were too. This however did not comfort her in any way, and in fact only added fuel to the flame of panic overcoming her body and mind. Feeling trapped and suffocated the girl began to squirm slightly, still laid flat out on her back. Her muscles began to contract and spasm randomly as if she was having a fit, and her limbs and torso began to contort. 'Is this it?' she thought to herself, 'is this my "eternity"?', remembering back to what the man on the sofa had told her previously about this reality being her eternity. This made sense to the girl as she had felt an aura of knowing about the slothful man, even though his outward appearance and manner did not reinforce this feeling. She pushed again, this time more firmly, as firm as she could muster the strength to, on the door to her right. It didn't budge at all. She sighed, laid back flat on her back straight as a pencil and accepted defeat, finding shortly after that when you are able to accept your fate it becomes a lot easier to deal with. She even began to relax, fall asleep... no, not sleep, she still couldn't sleep, but something far more interesting was beginning to happen.

Speckles of multicoloured light began to appear from the darkness in front of her eyes. Speckles that quickly transformed into swathes. Ribbons of patterned multicoloured light consumed her vision as though she was tumbling through a kaleidoscope at an increasing pace. Suddenly her vision seemed to settle and come into gradual focus, starting as a small indiscernible image in the centre with faded edges, growing and spreading across her vision like the growth of a bacteria on a petri dish as the faded edges grew further apart revealing a clearer and bigger image within. A girl, blonde, slim, with facial features that couldn't be made out, blurred into one creepily featureless face by the girl's consciousness. It was herself, she could feel it. Once again she was looking at herself through some sort of transcendental vision. Again the girl seemed in some distress in the vision, fretting over an important decision, perhaps. Around the girl, seated on her bed in the middle of a plain room, all details of which completely blurred and indiscernible, sat a few bookshelves, the books upon them few and far between. Growing increasingly distressed, the girl in the vision placed her head in her hands and began to sob. Before long her sobbing turned into an angry scream, her fingers curled and fingernails dug into the top of her forehead just under her hairline, and with a second almighty scream of frustration the girl pulled downward on her skin maintaining the insertion of her fingernails above her brow, ripping the skin off of her face as she pulled it down to her chin. Gruesomely, she left the big mask-like flap of skin hanging only by the chin, dangling below her face, dripping with blood. Left behind was a bloodied semi-muscular face split right down the middle into two halves. Although indescribable with words, the left side appeared to be a face of good, purity, and the right evil, pure evil. Blood pulsed out gently around the edges as the muscles contracted in rhythm was the beat of a heart.

Snap! At the click of a finger the girl's vision returned to complete darkness. She screamed, and immediately grabbed her face with both hands, checking her skin remained. Thankfully it did, and she was back, lying on the floor in the boarded up room. Before she even had time to begin to digest the experience she had just had and to assess its meaning, she began to experience a rather severe itching sensation at the back of her legs, lower back and arms. Her instinct was to itch them, so she did, reaching first for the back of her upper left arm she scratched hard with her fingernails. Unexpectedly she felt her fingers brush away a small... thing, clinging to her upper arm. Assuming it to just be a small piece of inconsequential matter from the floor of the boarded up room, which presumably hadn't been opened up or cleaned for a long time, so this made sense. Then sitting up slightly to reach for the underside of her calves, the girl noticed an unsettling squirming and scuttling underneath her lower back. Stretching out and reaching under her calves the girl's hand was plunged into what seemed like a pile of bugs. Cockroaches, crickets, woodlice, whatever they were, they scuttled about frantically and individually while yet moving as one wave of tiny beasts, which the girl noticed, at another snap of the finger, were covering the entirety of the floor beneath her in one layer. Horrified, the girl reacted by immediately pushing on the door again with as much force as she could muster, but again to no avail. She frantically scrambled around behind her head hoping to find something of use to her. To her relief her fingertips came across the cold metal handle of the crowbar that she had brought in with her and forgotten about. Still in a frantic scramble the girl first attempted to pry open the door with the crowbar, but awkward positioning and lack of leverage made this a fruitless task. She resorted to hitting the door as hard as she could with the sharper end of the metal instrument. The banging rang in her ears with each weak-armed thud until at last it was accompanied by a slight wood-splitting sound together with the first beam of light piercing through the slightest hole in the door. Encouraged by her progress she continued to punch through the hole making it larger, still using the metal tool. As the hole grew bigger and more light entered, more sickening creepy-crawlies became visible, scurrying around and through the splintered hole she was creating. Her whole body was now consumed by a furious itch, only made worse by her desperate nature, which in turn made her even more desperate, the two interlinked in a truly vicious cycle.

Eventually the girl broke a whole big enough to squeeze through, not without getting considerable scrapes, scratches and splinters down both of her sides from armpit to hip, but she was simply desperate to escape the bug-infested room. She dragged herself out into the bathroom onto the neatly tiled floor, turned and looked at the hole she had just passed through. Not only was it puzzlingly small and splintered, a biblically horrifying amount of bugs proceeded to pour out of it. Some black, some brown, some with wings, some without, and with any combination of numbers of pairs of legs and eyes, they began to consume the bathroom in one consistent wave, spreading from the hole like a deadly disease. Her top now torn nearly into shreds and blood leaking from her in more places than it seemed worth thinking about. Now another treacherous decision lay upon her, remembering that any of the house members, all of which had seemed to entirely lose their previously welcoming mood, could be waiting for her on the other side of the door. Pausing for a moment and attempting to calm herself with long, deep breaths, the girl closed her eyes and thought about the visions she had experienced once again. Though impactful, the girl still struggled to find much meaning in the visions, yet a sense of optimism grew within her as she felt that there was purpose to what she was experiencing. She felt as though she could help the girl in the visions, herself, and that she had only just begun in her efforts to do so. A quick look down at her brittle-nailed and bruised hands reminded her of the beautiful gem upon her finger, and at once she knew, or more accurately she felt, what it was she should do. Run.

IX. Castle in the Sky

Flinging open the bathroom door it was to her almighty relief that none of the house's occupants were to be seen. Instead, the corridor displayed her exit route in a straight line in front of her like it was specifically designed for that purpose, dimly lit by two flickering lights like that of a night-time runway. Although not noticing anything remarkable about the flaky-painted white wooden outline of the lounge door frame on the left at exactly half the way down the corridor until she had reached it, the girl was momentarily stopped in her tracks as her body became level with it on her sprint down the long internal alley. Going from inconspicuously dull and dim, matching the rest of the corridor, to a ferociously burning supernova of hell at the drop of a hat, the lounge featured a roaring fire, burning so bright and hot that the entirety of the girl's left side felt as though it immediately burnt, the skin tightening and even beginning to crack. In front of the fire, which despite its power was somehow still contained to the box shaped recess in the back wall of the lounge, sat all of the members of the house. Some on the stools, some simply kneeling in front of it as if bowing to its almightiness. All completely transfixed on the flames, like it was their god, they appeared to worship it without moving their lips or blinking their eyes even once. The girl also noticed the clock above the fire, of which both hands were now on 'VI'. As soon as the house members began to slowly turn their heads, once again in complete eerie unison, the girl decided without hesitation not to wait for them to complete their gut-wrenching rotations. Resuming her sprint down the corridor and into the front room, the girl once again envisaged the books she had found in the library, which by now she had concluded must surely be clues to her situation, alongside the intense visions she had sporadically experienced. Remembering one book specifically, 'Heaven and Hell', the girl's body tensed up as she began to accept the possibility that this was what she was experiencing – heaven, and hell. Assuming this to be the case, the girl, for the first time knew what she was going to do. Upon entering the front room the girl was again stopped momentarily as sat in the centre of the front room was a long thin table with wheels and leather buckles and straps fixed to its top, like some sort of medieval torture device. 'Is this for me?' she thought, panickedly. Again a flashback from a vision hit her of herself being strapped to what she thought was a bed by leather buckles and straps, with the house members surrounding her. These flashbacks were seemingly becoming more frequent and making her whole mental state more turbulent, like she was tossing and turning, unable to escape a bad nightmare. Only for a split second did the girl imagine quite how uncomfortable it would be to lay upon the hard wooden surface of that table, let alone being strapped down by your wrists, ankles and neck by brutish rudimentary leather straps. In the next moment the girl was out the front door. At this point the girl almost dragged her sorely bruised and slashed legs across the sharp gravel to the edge of the floating island. With the sky now filled with an evil redness and an almost unbearable heavy heat in the air, the girl turned to look at the house before taking one courageous backward step off of the edge. The grass gently tickled the underside of her feet as she stepped backward across it, and the house, despite what it had done to her, at this moment looked rather peaceful and apologetic. As she fell fatefully past the layers of grass, soil, and then rock, which came to a sharp tail at the island's bottom, the girl was forced to seriously consider if she had made the right decision.

Printed in Great Britain
by Amazon